THE
DEADLY
DANCE

THE
DEADLY
DANCE

CORA TAYLOR

*For Sara Loumantarakis
The Perfect Roomie!
Cora Taylor*

COTEAU BOOKS
WWW.COTEAUBOOKS.COM

Edited by Geoffrey Ursell.
Cover illustration by Aries Cheung.
Cover and book design by Duncan Campbell.
Printed and bound in Canada at Marc Veilleux Imprimeur Inc.

National Library of Canada Cataloguing in Publication Data

Taylor, Cora, (date)
The deadly dance / Cora Taylor.

 ISBN 1-55050-272-7

1. Time travel—Juvenile fiction. I. Title.
PS8589.A883D42 2003   jC813'.54   C2003-910868-6
PZ7.T21235De 2003

10 9 8 7 6 5 4 3 2 1

401-2206 Dewdney Ave
Regina, Saskatchewan
Canada   S4R 1H3

available in Canada and the US from:
Fitzhenry & Whiteside
195 Allstate Parkway
Markham, Ontario
Canada   L3R 4T8

The publisher gratefully acknowledges the financial assistance of the Saskatchewan Arts Board, the Canada Council for the Arts, the Government of Canada through the Book Publishing Industry Development Program (BPIDP), and the City of Regina Arts Commission, for its publishing program.

*To my grandson Dylan Livingston,
who loved Crete too.*

One of the most interesting finds in the excavation of the Minoan Palace of Knossos in Crete is the fresco of a young man somersaulting over the back of a charging bull. A lithe young woman waits behind the bull to help in his landing, while yet another boy or girl grasps the animal's horns, preparing, it appears, to make a similar somersault. This scene is repeated on pottery, statues, and other artifacts from that time. There is no doubt that during Minoan times there was a sport or ritual involving a bull. But there is never any sign of weapons or of any intention to kill or harm the bull. If there was a sacrifice involved, it was not the animal that would die.

Always the scene is the same. A youth – part of a team of both young men and women – takes the bull by the horns as it charges and somersaults over its back. Is this another case of legend blending with fact? In the myth of Theseus, seven youths and seven maidens are sent from Athens to Crete to be sacrificed to the Minotaur. Could they have been a team of bull dancers? Many scholars – from Cottrell to Renault – have believed this might be true. At any rate, it is obvious that the bull dancers existed, and were part of the ancient Minoan civilization.

CHAPTER ONE

It was just a movement. For a moment she'd remembered the painting: the fresco of the Bull Dancers, acrobats of the bull games, in the museum. And now – here in the palace where it had all happened so long ago – she'd started to swing into the vault. She hadn't done it of course. Too many people. She shouldn't even have tried that bit, the opening to a forward flip. What had gotten into her, made her do it?

But suddenly, in the flash of a moment, everything had changed. This tour through the ruins, all these people, had disappeared. And there'd been dust and noise in the bright sunshine and the bull charging towards her....

Now it was all back. She was standing here, in the tour group at Knossos as they clustered obediently around the umbrella-toting guide, listening to her speech. "The palace had twelve hundred rooms and was occupied by two thousand people. And," she paused, "we have uncovered three sets of plumbing pipes: pipes to bring in fresh running water from the hillside over there, pipes to drain and collect the rainwater in cisterns, and pipes to remove the sewage. And..." Another pause, longer this time, "...and we have so far uncovered... five...flush...toilets!" The Guide looked around dramatically as if she were personally responsible not only for their excavation but also the original construction. "No doubt more will be found."

Penny stood trying to collect her thoughts as the group moved on.

The noisy shouts, the background roar of crowds and the bull were gone. But the smell of it still lingered in her nostrils somehow. The dust and the animal smell – the bull, strong with dung and sweat. And stronger than anything the scent of fear – her own.

Penny pushed through the crowd to lean against a pillar. She was dizzy, but she was used to that. She really should have eaten some of the breakfast back at the hotel. Now the heat and the bus trip and all the standing and waiting had made her feel dizzy. That must be it. She'd been weak and had hallucinated the whole thing. It scared her. Weak and dizzy she could handle, but she hadn't experienced anything quite like this before.

She never ate breakfast anyway. She used the

excuse that she was always in a hurry. Would rush through the kitchen, grab a glass of milk and take a few glugs to satisfy her mother and then plead lateness. Food definitely didn't appeal to her in the morning. Here in Crete, at the hotel, it was a sort of buffet of everything from scrambled and boiled eggs and all sorts of meat, to cheeses, tomatoes and cucumbers, several kinds of bread, croissants, cereal, and desserts of all sorts. Too much to even look at.

Her father had loaded his plate, looked hopefully at her and said, "Might as well eat up – we're paying for it anyway!"

She'd smiled dutifully. Dad always trying to get a bargain – the family joke. "Breakfast Included" on the hotel brochure would appeal to him. And he'd get his money's worth or be darned. Looking at his plate piled high with eggs, bacon, and at least a dozen tiny sausages almost finished her off. Not that her mother's plate was much better. Not piled high but filled with things Penny could never associate with breakfast – feta cheese, tomatoes, tiny black olives. Not her idea of breakfast even if she could have eaten. She had taken some of the fruit and a croissant just to please her father. She was trying.

This was an expensive trip, probably blew the holiday budget for the next few years, and even though they were pretending it was for her mother, who'd studied Classics at university back home in Edmonton and had always wanted to come here, she said, Penny knew that it was mostly to get her away. That's why they'd left Tom behind even though they claimed it was because he had hockey camp he couldn't miss. Leaving him, they'd hoped to avoid the screaming fights that she and her older brother constantly had. Fights that left Penny crying and shaking with rage so that she'd end up in the bathroom "barfing her guts out" as Tom so delicately expressed it.

Not having him around had really helped, it was true. Her parents were falling over themselves trying to make her have a good time. The least she could do was fake it.

She could hear the concern in her mother's voice as she rushed back. "Are you all right, Dear? I thought you were lost!"

Penny realized that the tour had moved on without her. She pulled herself together. "No problem, Mum." She smiled, and moved along beside her mother to catch up as the tour guide led everyone into the next room.

"Don't let on – don't show your weakness." Isn't that what Coach said? "Use your inner strength...there is always more than you think." She couldn't spoil this trip; it was her mother's dream, even though Penny knew they'd never have taken it if it hadn't been for her. A big sacrifice to get her away. And she knew that they were going to have to do something big for Tom because hockey camp just didn't measure up to a trip like this. He'd hold out for the cash equivalent, Penny was sure. There must be a bribe going on because after the first major blow-up when the trip was announced, he'd remained sullenly silent.

She wondered idly when she'd come to hate her older brother. With just the two of them one might have thought they'd form some kind of alliance, but she couldn't remember anything beyond barely enduring his presence and relief whenever he left the house. For the first time, she wondered if he felt the same about her.

This trip had proved one thing, if nothing else – she could get along with just her parents around. The knots in her stomach seemed to be untying themselves, not like at home, when she could feel them tighten each time she walked into the house.

CHAPTER TWO

They left the palace and made their way toward the buses. Her dad stayed behind talking to the tour guide as Penny and her mother climbed aboard.

She was trying to listen as her mother told the story of Theseus and the Minotaur, but her mind kept slipping back to the crazy hallucination she'd had back on the tour. The noise, the bull charging and the smell. So real, so *there*.

"Each year as tribute," her mother was saying, "Aegeus, King of Athens, had to send seven youths and seven maidens to Crete to sacrifice to the Minotaur, the half-man half-bull monster who had been born to Queen Pasiphae with the bull Zeus sent...."

Penny knew the story of the Minotaur, most of it anyway. Her mother's voice seemed to have a lulling effect, as if she were reading a bedtime story. Penny couldn't have paid attention anyway; she had other things on her mind.

It had been so brief. Like the moment of illumination when lightning flashes at night and suddenly everything appears, clear and bright, but then is gone before you can blink or look around. She tried to remember, but her eyes had told her little except the bull coming towards her. There'd been the smell, but sound too. Shouts from people nearby, people she had not glimpsed but whose voices had been near enough to stand out. And in the background, the roar. A crowd. Not the sedate cheering she'd heard at gymnastic competitions. Louder. Like what? A hockey game? Different from that. Louder and fiercer. When there was a fight. Yes, more like what you heard when Dad watched a boxing match on TV. She wondered if it was the same as at a bullfight. A blood sport. The roar of a crowd knowing that something or someone would die.

"And then Ariadne, King Minos' daughter, gave him a ball of twine, so that he could find his way out of the labyrinth after he had killed the Minotaur." Her mother paused to see if Penny was really listening. "Did you know that it was called a 'clew' in Greek, which was where our word *clue* comes from?"

Penny shook her head. That was interesting. A clew to find your way out of a maze. She liked that.

She'd been surprised to find that she understood quite a few Greek words, though her father seldom spoke it. He was becoming more fluent as the trip progressed. His mother had been Greek, but she had died when Penny was six.

According to family legend, her grandmother had spoken Greek to Penny and Penny had understood and spoken back. Apparently, after her grandmother died, Dad had tried to keep her going, but once she started school she'd always answered him in English. She didn't remember that at all.

She only had one memory of Yia-yia Chryssoulakis and that was a smell – a smell and a taste. A sweet sticky bun Yia-yia used to make. Penny shut her eyes. She could almost taste the memory. Sort of like a French pastry, but soft in the middle with something like lemon curd or custard that melted in your mouth. She breathed in. That was it! Cinnamon! She could smell it!

Too much! She was starting to lose it all right. Get a grip, Penny, she told herself sternly. She opened her eyes, and there right under her nose was the bun, and Dad holding it out and laughing.

"I thought you were asleep,"

Penny's eyes widened. Then she found herself laughing too. Partly relief at knowing she had not hallucinated again, and partly delight at Dad remembering how she'd loved those buns. It felt good to be sharing happiness, not just pretending.

"Bugatsa," she said softly, hesitantly, almost to

herself, and then laughed again at the shocked look on her father's face.

"You remembered? You were so little, but your Yia-yia used to make them for you. When I saw a vendor with a tray of them I couldn't resist." He shot a guilty glance at Penny's mother. "I figured I'd be in trouble with the germ patrol but..."

"I didn't say a word!" Her mother was defensive. "But really, all the flies and dust...."

Penny had already taken a bite. The soft melting centre was just as she remembered. She remembered, too, Yia-yia taking them from the oven and the awful wait for them to cool. Helping sprinkle the cinnamon and icing sugar on top, trying to get it just right, but always dumping too much, though Yia-yia never minded.

Germs or not, Penny ate every bit of the bun. She savoured every bite and then licked her fingers. She would savour the memory it evoked, too. Maybe the real memories would erase the strange scene she'd experienced with the bull. She wanted this unfamiliar feeling of happiness to last as long as possible. But even as she thought of it, she could feel her stomach tighten again, and hoped she would not have to ask the bus driver to stop so that she could throw up.

CHAPTER THREE

"You know, it really is ridiculous that we've waited so long to come here," Mum was saying the next day as the rented car buzzed up the narrow paved road. "I have always wanted to come here and you never even told me that your mother came from Crete...I mean I knew she was Greek, but you never said where."

They were headed for the village where Yia-yia had been born. Dad had recognized the name on the map, and suddenly it had all come out.

"But they left when she was hardly more than a baby. And all the family there immigrated to Canada. Once they got there, even if there had been money to go back, there was really no one left to visit. People didn't spend all that money to take trips like this just for pleasure..." His voice trailed off as he concentrated on steering the little green Hyundai up the narrow mountain road.

Penny let them argue. She would keep out of it. She concentrated on the scenery. It was certainly like nothing she knew in Canada. Rocky hillsides, the red earth of Crete soft in the sunshine, flowers blooming everywhere. And everywhere hairpin turns which the drivers of Crete ignored, passing each other anyway.

The car rental had been Mum's idea, and there'd been big resistance from Dad – of course. But he'd finally given in when Penny'd meekly suggested that it would be fun to get out of Heraklion and see some more distant parts of the island. Actually she was getting tired of just the sightseeing tours and the constant pressure of hotel meals – the way her parents kept urging her to eat was making her stomach knot up again.

It wasn't until they were poring over the road map this morning at breakfast that her father had noticed the familiar name. Really, Penny thought, it was wonderful that he remembered a name he'd probably only heard a few times long ago, like her remembering the *bugatsa*. But her mother was big on tracing family history and family trees, though they never saw much of her relations. It was as if they were easier to keep track of on paper. The Greek uncles and cousins were much more a part of life. Though since Yia-yia's death, they mostly only saw them for funerals and weddings every year or two, because the majority of them still lived in Toronto where Dad grew up.

The drive was wonderful, sun shining on hillsides and then more hillsides as the road wound up and down. It seemed to Penny it was mostly up, with a panorama of vineyards and olive trees stretching below. Was it her imagination or could she actually smell the olives, a warm heavy scent that floated through her open window? Dad had decided that it was too expensive to get the air-conditioned car and now that they were out of the city, Penny didn't mind. Larks were singing, sounding very like the meadowlarks from home, though they didn't sit on fenceposts so you could see what they looked like.

Now and then, when they were up beyond the fields, they could see a flock of the long-haired sheep and hear the tinkle of sheep bells. Shepherds carried crooks just like the ones in the Christmas story.

Everywhere there were lovely domed churches, some of them very old. What fascinated Penny were the miniature churches on posts along the roadside. She'd thought perhaps they were church mailboxes, until Dad explained that they were memorials to people who had been killed in that place, either in accidents or in the war. Then she felt sad when she saw so many, but she would try to catch a glimpse inside as they went by – she could see names and sometimes pictures and candles and flowers. The country cemeteries were still covered with the flowers people used to decorate their graves at Easter, making them look like masses of gardens or floats in a parade.

They came around a corner and there it was. What there was of it.

CHAPTER FOUR

They spent the rest of the day. Dad found an old man in black who was actually wearing one of the little fringed head bands Penny'd seen in stores sold as souvenirs. There had been old men sitting in the town squares or in front of tavernas and restaurants in every village they'd passed. Her mother kept saying how much nicer it was than shipping them off to nursing homes. Dad's man, Alekos, was about the same age as Yia-yia would have been if she were still alive, so he didn't remember her, but he did remember his parents talking about the family that had left for Canada.

"Their house was near ours up by the church." He pointed up the hillside. "Would you like to see it?"

So they trekked up. The old man walked very slowly which was fine with Penny. It gave her a chance to look around without feeling too nosy. There were wonderful old stone houses, some falling down, so you could see the old brick ovens, overgrown grass, and flowers like some amazing rock garden. Here and there a few chickens scratched in a yard and there were even some goats tethered in the empty spots around the edge of the village. Below them olive groves stretched. There were some new houses too, built like the others with stairs to the roof or upper part of the building, and lots and lots of flower pots. Penny enjoyed the walk though she wished her mother wouldn't be snapping pictures like a tourist at every turn in the road.

The house was small; the closest to it in Canada was probably one of the little lake cottages, like the ones she had seen at Sylvan Lake called "dun Roamin" or "bide-a-wee". But size was the only similarity. This was old. Made of weathered brick, it looked as though it would have been ancient when Yia-yia was born. Penny's mother took a million pictures: Dad and the house, Dad and Alekos and the house, Dad and Penny and the house, Dad and Penny and the old man and the house, and the house by itself from every conceivable angle.

"Just think, Penny, you'll be able to show these pictures to your grandchildren," she said happily as she snapped away.

Penny tried not to let her sarcasm show but

she couldn't resist a crack. "Right and I'll learn to make *bugatsa* too!"

Obviously, her mother hadn't noticed the tone and took her words at face value, for she stopped the incessant picture taking and came over and gave Penny a hug. It made Penny feel guilty to notice that there were tears in her mother's eyes.

Later as they wandered back to the car they stopped at a little taverna and had dolmades with feta cheese and olives. It was nibbling food which made Penny relax – no plate to clean up. She took a little and found herself enjoying it. Dad was babbling away in Greek to anyone who'd listen – delighted that the language was coming back to him – and Penny was surprised to find she understood most of the simpler sentences. It seemed so comfortable in the late afternoon sun that Penny hated to see it beginning to set. Not a dazzling prairie sunset like at home – here it seemed to fade into a haze, though with the mountains in the way she couldn't see it drop into the sea.

It was Dad who suggested that they stay at the little hotel they'd parked beside when they came into town.

"But we've *paid* for the hotel back in Heraklion!" Penny blurted without thinking, earning a kick in the shins from her mother.

"Crete has evidently made a changed man of your father," Mum laughed. "Quick, let's check in before he's himself again!" And she grabbed Penny's hand as they ran down the hill.

She slept fitfully. Dreamed of bulls and fierce cheering. The fresco at the museum come alive.

CHAPTER FIVE

Penny sat in the back seat of the car the next day, studying the road map. She hadn't noticed before but they'd be passing close to Knossos on the drive back to Heraklion.

"Dad, do you think we could stop at Knossos and look around some more...it would be nicer to do without a tour...without the crowd pushing along...?"

She stopped, surprised at herself. Two days ago she had been puzzled and frightened by the strange experience at Knossos. Did she really want to go back? It seemed her curiosity was stronger than her fear. Anyway if Dad said no, and he probably would, she wouldn't argue. It didn't matter, did it? She really didn't care, did she?

She hadn't counted on her mother's enthusiasm. "Oh, Penny! What a great idea! I've been wanting to do just that, trying to figure out how I could go through it again but I was afraid you and your Dad would be bored."

"You were right," he mumbled. But he gave in much more easily than Penny had expected. "Okay, I can see I'm outnumbered. Where do I turn off?"

Penny sat back. She noticed one of the many guidebooks her mother had brought along and found the floor plan of the palace. Exactly where had they been when she'd had that flashback? It hadn't been long after the throne room. The place marked "Central Court" probably. But surely that was not where the bull dancers performed. Wouldn't there be an arena, an amphitheatre – sort of like the one they'd seen at the Acropolis in Athens? The map didn't show anything. Perhaps it had been there in that courtyard then. She would look again.

She read from the guidebook. "As soon as you enter the palace of Knossos through the West Court, the ancient ceremonial entrance, it is clear how the legends of the labyrinth grew up around it. Even with a detailed plan, it's almost impossible to find your way around...." The best way to see it was just to wander around, the guidebook said.

"Taverna Ariadne," Penny read as they passed by a small cluster of shops – the guidebook referred to it as, "a string of pricey tavernas and tacky souvenir stands."

"Maybe you could stay there, Dad," she suggested brightly. "Find somebody to practise your Greek on!" She knew he didn't want to spend any more time looking around the palace, and it would leave one less person to cope with while she tried to find the place she'd been yesterday when she made the move.

"Yes, dear, why don't you explore a bit in the vicinity?" her mother agreed. "Give us a few hours and then come to pick us up."

"Right Dad...no point in paying another entry fee when you don't even want to go!"

So it was agreed, he'd pick them up at five o'clock when the place closed.

Once inside the gates, Penny felt a strange sense of urgency that she hadn't noticed before. All she wanted to do was find the room, but first she'd have to lose her mother. It turned out to be easier that she thought. For the first five minutes or so they followed a tour group, but Penny hated the crowd even more this time and she could tell Mum was annoyed by some of the dumb comments of the tourists.

"The guidebook says it's best to just wander around on your own...." she suggested. To her delight Mum grabbed her arm and they slipped into another area away from the group.

"Brilliant, Penny," she whispered. "I've always wanted to do this!"

Penny felt a little guilty. Her mother looked so happy and excited – like a kid let out of school. She kind of hated to suggest that they separate. She didn't have to.

"You know, I'd like to see if I can find the dolphin mural again. It's in the queen's chambers...the queen's Megaron, I think. Why don't we meet in an hour at Sir Arthur's head...I mean, if that's all right with you...I don't want to abandon you or anything..."

Now Mum was looking guilty but Penny didn't have to feign enthusiasm. "Hey! Great idea, Mum!" The tour guide had gone into a lengthy explanation about Sir Arthur Evans beside the bronze bust near the entrance. And her mother had given an even lengthier one about the archeologist who'd spent thousands of dollars – today it would be millions – of his own money excavating and rebuilding the palace. "Except I don't have my watch on so why don't we get together there as it's closing... that way I'll know because everybody will be leaving."

Penny watched her mother go. "Don't get lost, Mum!" she called. "Remember, we haven't a clew!" Exit laughing, she thought. She couldn't believe the feeling of exhilaration she had. Exhilaration, and something else. It was not unlike the way she felt before a competition. Excitement and a little fear. As she walked she realized that she needn't have worried about finding the right place. She didn't need a ball of twine to get her through the labyrinth. Somehow she seemed to know where she was going.

CHAPTER SIX

It worked! This time she'd been alone and carried the forward flip through perfectly. But Penny's instant of triumph at having succeeded was short-lived. There, directly in front of her, was the bull. Her somersault had brought her right in range of its horns.

All she could see was the huge white animal as he stood pawing the ground. The brightly painted horns seemed inches away, too close for her to begin another leap. And she was too frozen to turn and run.

Then someone came from behind her, flinging her aside with one arm. The next moment he was grasping the bull by the horns, then leaping into a brief handstand before he somersaulted over the bull's back to land on his feet. The crowd went mad! They cheered the young man as the bull stood momentarily confused, and then a girl a little older than Penny stepped forward and did a forward salto, leading the bull away from Penny.

Now she felt calloused hands grabbing her shoulders, pushing her into the background. It was him – the young man who'd leapt the bull in front of her. Penny pressed back as close to the wall as she could. She watched as the bull dancers moved in and out. She realized that there were a dozen or more of them working as a team. Always one behind the bull to catch the leaper when he came over the bull's back if the landing was poor or if he stumbled. Another member of the team stayed in motion, ready to distract the bull if he turned too quickly and caught someone with his horns. Something like a rodeo clown. Except the entire team moved constantly, poised and turning in a complex gymnastic routine. It *was* a gymnastic routine – except the "horse" was alive. And could kill.

These athletes would have earned tens at the Olympics, Penny figured. Except for them the medal was being alive when the routine was over.

So far only the boys had done the somersault over the back of the bull, but now a girl, small and brown-skinned, stepped forward and launched into a forward flip that brought her directly in front of the bull. For a moment she paused and the noise of the crowd seemed to stop too. Penny held her breath. Then, as the bull lowered his head, she grasped the horns and did a perfect handstand. Penny gasped. The crowd found its voice again.

The bull in his slow-thinking way had begun a charge just before she leapt. As the girl balanced it finally began to move and the momentum carried the jumper over his back. Obviously, this was how the routine was supposed to be done. But without a purpose to his charge the bull stopped suddenly, too suddenly for the girl to clear his back. She slid off the right rear haunch just as the bull turned to attack. Luckily she was quick and regained her footing while her teammates flipped and turned dangerously close in an effort to distract him. But the bull was not so easily distracted this time and before she could spin away his horn caught her on the shoulder, tossing her off balance. Penny watched in horror as a flower of blood appeared on the brown skin. Even before she realized that he was there, the young man who'd pushed her appeared. Somehow he caught the girl's hands and flipped her. Then she was flying out of the bull's line of vision to be caught by other teammates and moved past Penny to a narrow doorway out of the ring.

One by one the dancers followed, bowing their way out to the cheers of the crowd, until there was only the young man making his way gracefully towards the exit as the bull turned in confusion, pawing and snorting in the centre of the ring.

"Go!" the youth yelled at her. The language

was strange but there was no question what he meant. Penny slipped out and he followed.

The passageway was long and dark. Penny realized that it was probably one of the corridors she'd walked in the ruins, but then it had been open to the air, not nearly so ominous. As they moved along, the roar of the crowd faded and was gone. The youth brushed by her and ran ahead into a large chamber. Penny realized it was their equivalent of a locker room.

The smell of sweat and leather and even some of the musky smell of bull dominated the room. On a bench at the far side sat the girl who'd been injured. Someone, not one of the team, a servant or slave perhaps, held a basin, while another girl, one of the team, daubed at the wound. It still bled but didn't appear to be deep. From where she stood Penny could not see any sign that it had penetrated far enough to affect the muscle.

She edged silently along the wall, wishing she could disappear. She dreaded the moment when they would notice her, when the young man who'd saved her would wonder where she came from.

Right now he was striding over to the injured girl. There wasn't much sympathy in his voice. In fact he was downright angry with her. And whatever he was saying, whatever the words were, there was no question that she was being bawled out for something.

Penny assumed that he was captain of the

team and maybe coach too, if they had such a thing. She sympathized with the girl who sat there on the receiving end. When Coach lit into her like that, she wanted to die, dissolve – just shrivel up and disappear.

To Penny's surprise the girl looked up and seemed to be telling him off right back. Obviously a gutsy chick, but then look how she'd faced the bull. Maybe that made a difference. How scary could a coach be to somebody on this kind of team?

Penny caught herself smiling. Wouldn't she just love to take that girl back home and have her give Coach as good as she got. A taste of his own sarcastic medicine. Lovely.

Everybody seemed to be ignoring her, which was good. She lowered herself onto a bench and studied them.

The girls and boys were dressed much alike, in short leather kilts, more like loincloths wrapped around them, fastened somehow she supposed, since they hadn't flopped down during the handstands. Their chests were bared, the girls' firm young breasts without protection, though many wore heavy jewelled collars made of gold. Their faces were painted, their eyes heavy with mascara, and they wore calf-high boots of gilded leather. Penny wondered if barefoot would have been better, but she noticed the leather soles were soft like gym shoes. So perhaps for the coarse sand of the bullring, boots were better. Both boys and girls had long hair, twisted back and tied in ponytails.

Someone came through the passageway from the ring and announced something and the team rose as one and followed the captain and the injured girl back out into the hot sunshine. Penny followed too, as near as she dared.

The bull was gone and people stood and cheered as the team entered to a fanfare of trumpets. Some of the crowd threw flowers into the ring. From other doorways that Penny had not seen before, other teams appeared. Four in all.

The teams stood proudly as servants appeared with gifts as well as flowers for certain of the dancers. The injured girl received something that sparkled and flashed in the sunlight. She bowed to the place the servant pointed and draped the jewel on the wounded shoulder so that now the red badge framed it. So they did get medals, Penny thought.

She wondered how long they would have to stand here in the hot sun. She was feeling dizzy and the injured girl must be wishing to go back to the room and lie down.

As if they'd read her mind, the captains turned and led their teams back.

Penny slipped through the door behind her team wondering if anyone in the crowd had noticed her standing there, a girl in strange clothing. Never would she have believed that shorts and a tank top could look so completely foreign and wrong. Still, her shorts were gold coloured, not unlike the leather kilts of the team, and she was wearing a peach-coloured top – maybe from the stands it would look like skin. She almost laughed out loud. Here she was, wishing people would think she was half-naked so she wouldn't be conspicuous!

CHAPTER SEVEN

enny wondered as she followed the team if
she should just linger behind in the corridor and wait until the crowd left. Maybe
she could just do a backward flip and be back in
her own time. Wouldn't she startle a tour group if
she landed in their midst! But she'd really only
been here a few minutes and she wanted to learn
more about these bull dancers. They seemed to be
ignoring her anyway. Maybe they thought she was
just a slave who'd made a wrong turn. Actually she
hoped that wasn't true. Slaves probably got beaten
for that.

She thought she could slip in, sit quietly on
the bench as she had before, and just observe.
This time however she was barely in the door
when the young man, the captain – at least until
she found out differently that's how she would
think of him – strode over and began to scold her.

She knew that modern Greek was very different from the kind of Greek people took in university – classical Greek. But this was Crete over three thousand years ago: would they speak the same language? Probably not. The Minoans would have had their own language.

Even without knowing the language there was no mistaking the tone of voice. At least he wasn't quite as angry as he'd been with the girl. And she could detect that some of it was questions. "Where had she come from?" no doubt, and, "What the hell was she doing out in the ring?" Things like that. Penny shook her head. Gestured, "I don't understand." A gesture she realized might well be mistaken for, "I don't care." She hoped not.

Evidently he accepted the former, because he stopped and started over in a different language. Penny realized it was some form of Greek, since she recognized a word or two. But the accent was strange, nothing like what she'd been hearing on the streets. Still, that made sense. Like listening to somebody speak Old English. Or Chaucer stuff. Except that three thousand years ago, there hadn't been any English, not even Old.

Her mind was racing but all she could do was shake her head. He'll probably think I can't speak, she thought miserably.

Obviously that was what he did think. For he seized her chin and seemed to be trying to pry open her mouth. It was the sort of thing her stupid brother did if she refused to answer him when she got tired of his baiting and trying to start fights. Penny reacted without thinking.

"Hey! Lay off, you creep!" She exploded.

He jumped back and the others who'd been watching began to laugh. Penny felt a little silly. Maybe people actually had their tongues cut out and he was just checking. She was relieved to see that he was grinning too. He began to laugh, shrugged and turned to the others. "Bar-bar-oi," he said.

That she understood.

She had to confess that most of the time she didn't listen to her mother's little lectures – stories of myths and things about ancient empires like the Minoans, things Mum had learned in her Classics courses at University. They'd been going on a lot since they got here. But sometimes bits were neat. Interesting. Like the word *clew*.

And *bar-bar-oi*. Apparently it was what the ancient Greeks had called people whose language they couldn't understand. "Oi" meant people and "bar-bar" was just their word for "blah blah." Nonsense words. So it meant "people who babble" or actually, "people who don't speak Greek." It was where our word "barbarian" came from. Today it meant uncivilized and maybe to the Ancient Greeks anybody who didn't speak Greek was considered pretty uncivilized.

So, Penny thought, I'm a barbarian. She

smiled at the youth. Okay, I guess it's sign language for a while. Pointing to herself, she said slowly, "Penelope."

She never used her real name, even kept it off her class records after a grade one teacher had pronounced it "Penny-lope." But it *was* Greek and she tried to say it the way Yia-yia Chryssoulakis had. Maybe they'd even know the name. After all, as Mum never tired of pointing out, it was the name of Odysseus's queen, the one who'd waited so patiently even when it looked as if he was dead, it took him so long to return from Troy after the war. She wished she knew whether the Trojan War had been before or after the Minoan Empire.

The captain smiled, pointed to his chest and said, "Rhion."

Then one by one the others stepped forward, "Pylia," "Melanthro," "Alektryon," "Lukos," and "Keo."

Last of all the girl lying on the bench, her shoulder bound now with strips of white linen, raised herself. "Charis," she said and pointed, smiling weakly.

What now? Penny wondered. What happens to me now? Am I accepted into the team that easily? Does Captain Rhion assume I've been sent as a tribute from some defeated nation – a sacrifice to the bull like Theseus's Athenians? Just another *bar-bar-oi* come to die?

Apparently so, because when he led Penny away it was to a smaller roofed courtyard with vaulting horses – bulls? Definitely bulls, for they were built the size of bulls, with bullhide covers and bull-shaped heads topped by real horns. He paused at the doorway, led with a forward hand-spring into a vault, landed and turned, gesturing to Penny to follow.

She looked at him standing half-smiling, challenging her. He thinks I can't do it, she thought. How many years of gymnastics had it taken her to master something similar with the vaulting horse? Well if she was just some tribute slave, she would be able to do it. She'd show him.

She took a deep breath and began. She did it! The best vault she'd ever made. Maybe not quite as good as his, but she wished Coach had seen it. It might have kept him off her case for awhile.

She stood. Rhion nodded and then moved into another routine. This was strange to her and she stumbled in front of the fake bull. Before she could catch herself, she was twirled aside, the force of his grasp sending her in one direction while he somersaulted in another. It was a movement she remembered from the bullring. The idea was to confuse the bull so that his charge was slowed. Keep your eye on the bull, Rhion gestured – she assumed the words he was saying meant the same thing.

They practised for some time, until Penny

was starting to shake from exhaustion. Unlike Coach, Rhion let up when he saw her start to falter. He led her over to the bench and did the impossible – gave her a lecture on the various holds that were used when the bull dancers caught each other. Amazing. More like trapeze work – flyers' holds, Penny thought. Without understanding a word, though she could guess at a few, Penny learned by gesture and demonstration. When she didn't get it, she'd shake her head, look puzzled and he would smile and show her again. He was so patient. And strong. Kind too – just before they left to come here he'd gone over to the injured girl, Charis, and patted her shoulder and given her a little hug as she moved away.

Not the kind of coach Penny was used to. But then these were not the kind of athletes she was used to – life and death performances every time. She noticed a line of scar tissue on his brown chest, others here and there on his arms and side. Marks of glancing horns. Charis would have one on her shoulder when the wound healed. More than tribute jewels, these were the medals of the bull dancers.

Obviously the practice was over. Rhion patted her on the back in a friendly way, smiled and led her through another corridor.

The rest of the team were there already, boys and girls dressed alike, wearing short white tunics. There were platters of food on the table. Penny studied them curiously. The baked fish was recognizable but, being a prairie girl, Penny wasn't all that wild about fish. Still it might be the easiest to eat – the exercise had made her hungry. Maybe she could eat something.

Rhion picked up a piece of roast chicken and began to eat. Fingers were made before forks, she'd heard. Evidently it was true. Penny took a tiny piece of fish and nibbled at it. Quite tasty. She wasn't sure if it was the fish or the herbs it appeared to have been cooked in. She watched as Rhion picked up a flask, poured wine into a goblet until it was about a third full, then added water from another pitcher and handed it to her.

The exercise had made her thirsty so she took a sip. It was refreshing, not too strong. Better than the sip of retsina Dad had given her at the restaurant in Athens on their way here. This was tangy and yet smooth enough that you could almost taste the sunlight on the grapes. To her surprise it rested easily in her stomach. She reached for another piece of fish, ate it and tried a bit of the roast chicken. It wouldn't do for her to turn up to meet Mum half-sloshed.

And speaking of meeting Mum. She had no idea what time it was. Rhion had gone over to sit beside Charis who was reclining on a bench covered in pillows. Others were clustered around her talking excitedly. By the look of things they were replaying the events in the ring. What had gone wrong? Whose fault was it? How could it be avoided? Everyone seemed to have definite opinions. Nobody was looking her way Penny slipped quietly out of the room.

The bull court was deserted. The sand had been neatly raked. She waited, looking up to where the people had been sitting this afternoon to make sure there was no one there. Then, as closely as she could, she repeated the movement that had brought her here. Except this time she went from left to right instead of right to left.

CHAPTER EIGHT

I t worked! And luckily the courtyard was empty, though as she stood, a little breathless more from excitement than from the leap itself, Penny could hear a tour group approaching. She leaned against the wall as they entered and formed a neat cluster around the tour guide. It was good to hear a language she could understand again, even if she didn't care what they were saying.

"Excuse me," she said softly to a lady who backed up to lean beside her, "could you tell me what time it is?"

The lady was surreptitiously removing a shoe and rubbing her foot as she leaned. She waved her wrist in front of Penny's face.

It was only two o'clock. She'd been gone less than ten minutes! She could go back! There was still time to go back, now that she knew how easy it was to come back to the present. Penny couldn't wait for the group to move on.

She was halfway through the leap when she realized that there might be a bull in the ring again. The thought made her miss her landing and flop to the ground. Luckily she landed just inside the doorway to the bullring. Very luckily, for there was a black bull in the ring and a young man fallen. Penny watched in horror as the bull tossed the boy. She could see the teammates poised to catch him, others working hard to distract the bull. But it was not a clean toss. One horn had caught him in the belly and he fell gored and bloody at the feet of the bull.

She turned and fled down the corridor. She didn't want to see the rest. She didn't want to know who it was. And she was going to be sick.

She burst into the chamber, her hand over her mouth. She felt Rhion grab her and rush her to a basin in the corner. Outside, the music of the bull dance changed, became heavier and slower and then ended in a crescendo. She finished and collapsed on the bench nearby. The team were dressed for the dance. It must have been another team, the youth someone she had not met.

Melanthro and Alektryon rushed into the room. Penny realized they'd been watching what happened. The others turned and listened quietly as they described the death in the ring. Because she had seen the goring she found that she understood quite a bit of what they said. Rhion was questioning them and Penny realized that he was turning this into another lesson. The two witnesses had seen what led up to the accident; Penny had only arrived in time to see the awful end of it. Melanthro seemed to be playing the part of the doomed youth, while Alektryon was his partner. Someone had been caught out of position. But how could you predict the bull?

It was a new bull, new to the ring and to the team. She understood that much. And this bull gored to the left. With Lukos playing the part of the bull, Rhion danced in front of him, feinting always to the right, to straighten him. "Stay a little on the right," he said. "It is his weak side." He looked at Penny to see if she was understanding him. "Never be caught on the left of the horns with a bull like that." He acted out the words and she nodded.

Pylia came and handed her the leather kilted skirt with the tight cinch belt of the bull dancer. The leather was gilded so that it shone like gold. She measured her foot against Penny's; it was much smaller. While Penny put on the skirt the girl rummaged around in a large chest in the corner. They tried two or three pairs of the gilded boots before finding a pair that fit.

Now, Penny realized, it was time for the hard part. She was going to have to take off her top. Feeling miserable, she glanced around the room, shut her eyes and slipped it off. She was glad she wasn't wearing a bra. That would have really been strange to them. It took what felt like minutes before she dared open her eyes. She'd expected every boy in the room to be staring but nobody was. She realized this was what her mother meant by "cultural differences" – "What's strange in one society is often perfectly normal in another." Obviously that went for dress taboos too. She wondered what Mum would think of her con-forming to this "cultural difference."

The team was lining up and moving down the corridor. Penny fell into step beside Pylia. She noticed that Charis was not there. Obviously Penny was taking her place.

It was not until she entered the arena, felt the heat of the noon sun, and heard the music, that she remembered the boy who'd fallen. Her eyes went immediately to the spot and the pool of blood darkening in the sun. A wave of nausea swept over her and she stopped. Pylia grabbed her and pulled her on. Rhion led them to the centre of the court where they formed a circle facing the crowd. There was cheering especially for Rhion and then the music changed to a fanfare as, in one of the corners to Penny's left, a gate opened and the bull trotted in. To her relief it was not the black bull the other team had been working with but the white one she'd seen before.

The team spread out facing the bull, then

Rhion saluted it, and moved forward. Obviously, the bull had to be "danced" into the centre of the ring to give them space to move and without becoming trapped against the walls of the ring. The bull had stopped, head lowered. These first moves would be the most dangerous for the bull could not be vaulted as he stood.

On either side of Penny, dancers started to move, gracefully cartwheeling to the right and left of Rhion, but always staying behind him, letting him watch the bull. Everyone was shouting instructions to one another. Penny was pretty sure that Pylia's shout to her as she flipped away was, "Stay there!" Anyway that was what she did. And she heeded Rhion's advice.

Had she not been watching the bull, she would have missed his signal, for his hoof raked the ground only once before he began his charge. Rhion was ready, grasping the painted horns and swinging up over the bull's head. Now there was room behind the animal for him to complete his vault, using the bull's momentum to clear and land cleanly. He might have done it without a "catcher" but Melanthro had moved in and was ready to steady his captain. They turned the manoeuvre into a catch and let it move them around to the either side of the bull. Now two of the girls had flipped in front of the bull, which had stopped its charge in confusion. Rhion and Lukos came from either side, vaulting the bull sideways and landing perfectly in unison.

"Penelope!" Pylia called and they went into a routine that kept them out of range of the bull. Two of the other girls were doing the same thing on the other side of the court. It was like a tightly choreographed routine. Rhion and his partner once again vaulted the bull, but the beast turned right this time, veering toward Rhion before he had completed his landing. Without thinking, Penny ran forward and did a somersault in front of the animal.

Then there was a moment of stark fear as she wondered what she would do next. She was close enough to smell the rank bull smell, to feel the flecks of foam that dripped from his muzzle. A second flip perhaps, but could she get out of the bull's way fast enough? Not likely. However, Rhion had recovered now, and Penny's move had straightened the bull so that Rhion could come in, grasp its horns and do a hand stand. This time there was no momentum of a charge to carry him over, and he had come from a standing start. How would he land?

For a moment Penny stood stock still, afraid to breath. The crowd was screaming so much that she could hardly hear her teammates as they constantly shouted instructions to one another. She had never seen such teamwork. Rhion would have to come down beside the bull but there were now two teammates on either side, one to catch him and one to deal with the bull if that happened to be the way he turned. Rhion flipped to the right and was caught safely again.

Penny wished it would finish. It occurred to her that she was in the bull court and if she made the reverse move she might very well end up back in her own time, wandering though Knossus without a shirt on. The thought stopped her in her tracks and only Pylia calling got her moving again.

It was not long before it was over. The bull was making short confused charges but most of the time he would stand shaking his head pawing the ground. One by one the dancers moved to the side as they had the last time, leaving Rhion and two others vaulting from side to side, never letting the bull face them. Until he just shook his head and stood his sides heaving, tired and confused. Then everyone left, moving down the corridor.

Rhion came up beside Penny as they left the noise and heat behind. She was afraid he was going to scold her as he had Charis. She wasn't sure she should have made that foolhardy move, even though it had seemed to work and distract the bull. He didn't say anything, just put his arm around her shoulder and gave her a squeeze.

That was enough. She could not wait for the return to the ring and the bowing to be over. Even though this time, when the servants came forward with the special gifts, Rhion turned and bowed to her and placed one of his gifts in her hand, thanking her again. It was a tiny golden bull – like a charm for a bracelet.

She sat on the bench, pulling off her boots and slipping back into the sandals she'd bought in Athens.

Now it really was time to get back. A thought had suddenly occurred to her. What if, when the lady had told her the time, it was the right time but the wrong day? It might be two o'clock – tomorrow! She had definitely been gone longer than half an hour, more like three or four. So, what if time moved differently in the past, not the same as it was passing in the present? Instead of hours in the past being minutes in the present, it could just as easily be the opposite – hours in the past could be days in the present. Maybe it was 2:30, some time next week!

Her parents would be worried sick. She had to get back as soon as possible.

CHAPTER NINE

Penny left as soon as they went to eat. This time the platters of food only made her feel queasy. Charis was there and once again the centre of attention, so it was easy to slip away. Again the bull court had been freshly raked. Before she went into her move she stooped and took a handful of the coarse sand, letting it trickle between her fingers into the pocket of her shorts.

Again the move worked. This time she bumped into a large woman who was just leaving at the tail end of her tour. Luckily she hadn't been looking behind her, so she was only angry at being bumped, not shocked at someone appearing from nowhere.

"I'm so sorry..." Penny blurted. Actually she was glad it was somebody sturdy and not a frail elderly person she might have knocked down.

The woman glared at her. "There's no need to be in such a rush."

"I know...and I am truly sorry...but I was supposed to meet my mother and I don't know what time it is and I'm afraid I'm late." Sometimes the truth comes in handy, Penny thought. "Could you please give me the time?" Penny would have liked to ask for the date too, but that would have sounded ridiculous.

Grudgingly the woman looked at her watch. "It's a little after four," she said. "Ours is the last tour before the place closes."

"Thank you very much." Penny realized she could linger with the group and still be in time to meet Mum, but she really didn't want to hang around this lot. The woman still looked angry, although it occurred to Penny as she moved away that maybe that was a permanent expression and had nothing to do with being bumped into. Maybe she'd been one of those children whose mother had said, "if you make a face like that it will freeze that way," and it had actually happened! Penny nearly laughed out loud as she pictured the cross woman as a nasty-faced little kid.

At least she was smiling as she "excuse-me"d her way through the crowd and out of the chamber. The sun was still warm and she moved over to sit on a low wall that held the heat and felt comfortable against her legs. She knew that much of this building, and all of the chambers with roofs, were actually reconstructions by the archeologist Evans. But, from what she'd seen, the originals seemed quite similar, except that everything was brightly painted. Garish, almost. Of course she'd only been in the rooms the bull dancers used. No doubt the chambers of the nobles and royal family were lavish beyond any royal dwelling today. Judging by the jewellery they gave the bull girls and boys who pleased them, they'd had wealth beyond her wildest dreams.

She watched the tour group come out, the guide leading them toward her. Time to go. She'd stay ahead of them. She began to go, turned a corner and realized there was somebody ahead. A familiar walk, the short blonde hair.

"Mum!" she yelled, running forward. "You're here!"

Only now did Penny realize how much she had feared that this might be the right time but the wrong day or even week. She hadn't wanted to pursue the thought of what her parents might be going through over the disappearance of their daughter.

Mum was laughing, "Of course I'm here! Where did you expect me to be?"

Penny had run up and given her a hug. Her mother looked pleased but puzzled by the unusual show of affection. It had been totally an impulse and now Penny felt awkward and silly. She bent to undo her sandal, pretending to remove a pebble.

They walked on together. "So, dear, did you find anything interesting?"

Now what was she going to say? She really hadn't seen anything of the ruins except the last few minutes. And if she didn't say anything, Mum would be giving her the third degree in a minute. The best thing to do was to distract her, get her talking about something to do with the Minoans. Penny blurted the first thing that came into her head.

"I'm wondering about the bull leapers," she said. "Like the ones on that mural at the museum."

Her mother brightened. "Oh yes, the youths and maidens who danced for the bull...the doomed dancers." Penny had succeeded all right. Mum loved to talk about stuff like this. "I suppose the ancient Minoans had it over the Romans who just massacred people in their arenas for sport. Even the gladiators didn't have much chance of survival beyond days or perhaps weeks." She paused and quoted, "*Te morituri salutant!*"

"What does that mean?" Penny interrupted.

"We who are about to die salute you!" said Mum raising her arm dramatically, "It's Latin...it was what the gladiators said to the Emperor when they entered the ring."

Penny thought of Rhion saluting the bull like that as he went toward it, and of the youth impaled by the bull's horn earlier. Suddenly a chill swept over her and the day was no longer warm. Involuntarily, she hugged herself. That reminded her of the way Rhion had squeezed her shoulder in that little thank-you hug. She wondered what would have happened if she had not been there, if no one had been there at the key moment. Something like that must have happened to the boy who died.

"At least the Minoans recognized the grace and beauty of the bull dance – it was, after all, sort of a religious ceremony honouring the god Poseidon, and I suppose that the more talented ones might survive for months, maybe a year...," Mum paused thoughtfully, "...but I doubt any of them ever grew old."

Penny couldn't speak to respond. She should have known that. The doomed dancers, her mother had called them. Rhion and his beautiful talented team – even they were doomed? It was too much.

Luckily the talk had led them out of the palace area. Mum was waving. "Look there's your father. Right on time, of course!"

Penny sat very still in the back seat, thinking. From time to time her eyes filled with tears. It was a good thing her mother had something to say and Dad had enjoyed himself immensely. He even wanted to go back and eat at the taverna another day.

CHAPTER TEN

Penny did not sleep well that night. Her dreams were filled with dying dancers caught on the bull's horns, trampled in the dust, and with music crashing to a close.

Worse, her dreams filled with people she knew. Pylia, who'd guided her in the ring. Melanthro, standing by to catch dancers after their vaults. Charis, wearing her badge of blood so bravely. And Rhion, mostly Rhion – the feel of his arm around her, the grateful squeeze of her shoulder and his patient teaching to save her from making mistakes with the bull. The dreams always ended with a goring – not the young man who'd died in the ring today but someone else, some faceless friend – and her fear of knowing who. Worse still, somehow she seemed to be watching from the stands so the dying dancer could be anyone from the team – even herself. And she

would waken and lie sweating in the darkened
hotel bedroom. Reminding herself that it was
now, that she was here. And that the worst she
had to fear was going home to the humiliation of
Coach's criticism and her brother's cruel teasing.

She lay awhile, restless, until the sheets were
tangled about her feet. But even if she had been
able to, she was afraid to sleep again just now with
the dreams so fresh.

At last, when she had lain awake over an hour
and it was still only 2:30 by the clock on the bed-
side table, she got up and slipped into her shorts
and top against the night chill. She would do
what she did at home when she couldn't sleep at
night. Exercise. Practise until she was so tired she
could fall asleep before her mind wiggled through
the exhaustion to haunt her again. At home she
would go down in the basement and skip rope,
but she had no rope so she would just try some
limbering-up exercises.

She began slowly, stretching and bending,
careful to be noiseless although she was sure the
rooms were fairly soundproof. She'd noticed that
the only noise seemed to come from people in the
hall. People greeting each other loudly in German,
from the many tour groups that stopped at the
hotel. She was sure that even if she panted and
thumped a bit it wouldn't be noticed by her parents in the room next door. The marble floor was
cold on her bare feet but she kept moving, running

on the spot, until it didn't bother her anymore.

It was when she finally tried a handstand, and felt the sand trickling over her from inside her pocket, that she felt some alarm and tried to right herself.

Too late.

It was dusk in the bull court, the stands empty, and she was all alone. For a minute she stood absorbing the peace under the darkening sky. Then she saw Pylia running towards her. Anxious. Scolding a little, she grabbed Penny's arm and hurried her towards the changing room.

Penny understood some of it. She was obviously late for something. Not the bull dance, or even practice, for it was nearly night. When they entered the room, the girls stood together behind a tall woman wearing the tight bodice and tiered skirt of the Minoan females. On her wrists and on her arms above the elbows were heavy golden snake bracelets. Penny studied their jewelled eyes carefully as the woman spoke to her in a harsh scolding voice. Evidently she was in charge of the girls. By day they practised and ate and talked and danced for the bull, just as the boys did. But at night they were kept separate, guarded by this formidable woman. Penny noticed the coiled snake decorations on her cap and silently nicknamed her Medusa. Luckily, the woman turned away just as Penny felt a smile trembling on her lips at the thought.

They fell into step two by two, following the woman. Penny was last in line, with Pylia, and she turned to glance behind her, catching Rhion watching and waving. For me! she thought, pleased. But then as she turned again, she saw Charis ahead of her looking back too. Of course. For Charis. After all, she had been here longer, they were closer, and Penny remembered his concern for her when she was hurt. For Charis.

She felt Pylia take her hand and squeeze it. How strange that even without language she could feel such communication, such friendship from someone. Did she have a friend at home like this? Someone who sensed and cared so much? Not really. She was a bit of a loner. Maybe sharing life and death in the ring forged closer bonds than sitting behind someone at school. Penny smiled gratefully at Pylia. She would have hugged her but didn't want Medusa to scold again.

They were taken to a room not unlike the dressing chamber, except for a mural of shells and sea creatures similar to the dolphin piece her mother liked so well in the queen's room. No dolphins, but starfish and triton shells, and everywhere the spirals she'd seen on early Minoan pots in the museum. A less dramatic mural perhaps than the dolphins, but the same beautiful blue background. This one didn't survive, Penny thought. What a shame.

"Here," Pylia said, pointing to a narrow cot in

the alcove, "for you." Penny pointed to a similar one across from it. "For you?" Pylia laughed and nodded.

There was another room nearby with a large tub, the size of a six-person jacuzzi. Some of the girls were already in it, laughing and soaping each other while servants stood by with pitchers of water to wash away the soap. Penny couldn't help but look wonderingly at the pitchers. Had any of them survived to be glued together by an archeologist? The long, almost teapot-like spouts were similar to many of the pitchers she'd seen at the museum.

After their bath they changed into short white tunics and got ready to follow Medusa again. Penny noticed that the servants were gathering up the soiled clothes and darted back to slip her shorts and top under the mattress of her narrow bed.

She arrived back breathlessly to drop in line beside Pylia who only looked at her, smiled and shook her head.

They followed Medusa, down steps that appeared to be cut into the rock, to winding corridors deep beneath the palace. Penny and Pylia followed the other girls by the flickering light of the lamps some of them carried. Suddenly Penny was aware of someone following her. Someone else dressed like Medusa had fallen in behind her, not a woman but a girl about Penny's age. She too carried one of the little pottery oil lamps.

It seemed to Penny that they walked a very long way, but perhaps it was just the winding corridors and their slow pace that made it seem long. They came out only once, briefly, their little procession lit by the moon, before they moved into the shelter of a cave. Penny dared a look back. The palace shone in the moonlight below them. All that time the tunnel had been slanting upwards bringing them here. She'd noticed some incline but had not realized how much until now.

It seemed even darker at first in the cave after the moonlight outside, but soon they turned to enter a larger cavern. Obviously the shrine of the goddess. The floor at one end was covered with beautiful stone vases and statues glowing in the lamplight. In the background, an intricately-carved screen of latticework snakes hid the far end of the cavern.

Penny remembered her mother going on about the little statues of the goddess of the snakes and how they were really priestesses of the Earth Mother who was worshipped by the ancient Greeks. The Minoans honoured the Earth Mother Dia and the sea god Poseidon, which made a lot of sense, come to think of it. Especially when you lived on an island depending on the produce of land and sea. Her mother had gone on to give her a long lecture about how the myths, especially the conquests of the heroes Theseus and Heracles, were really allegories to explain the over-throwing of the ancient female goddesses by the male gods of the mainland Greeks.

So Medusa, her Medusa here, not the one in the myth, was a priestess. Maybe the legendary one was too, and Heracles killing her was just another case of wiping out an ancient shrine of the snake goddess. The snakes were sacred to the Earth Mother because they lived closest to the earth.

Penny liked snakes. Her cousin Katy had a pet python named Monty and Penny like to wrap him around her neck when she visited Katy and her brothers. Snakes' skin wasn't slimy like some people thought; it was dry and cool and Monty would slide around her shoulders and arms as smooth and soft as a caress.

The two priestesses, Medusa and the girl who'd walked behind, moved forward now, while the bull girls stayed back forming a semicircle with Penny and Pylia at the centre. Now in the flickering light another priestess, an old woman wearing a high headdress and a live snake about her waist, came from behind the screen. Two of the girls were carrying offerings which they came forward to give to the young priestess. She passed them to Medusa, who passed them to the old woman. The gifts were taken behind the screen. Then Medusa and the younger woman each took a side of the screen and rolled it back into the darkness. All the time the women were chanting something in the low growling words of some ancient language.

Penny tried to copy the respectful stance of Pylia and the other girls but her nose started to itch from the heavy smell of the perfumed oil and she feared she would sneeze. Luckily, she was distracted. The old priestess reappeared and the young one came and took Pylia and herself by the hand and led them forward.

Penny felt a surge of panic. Were they to be sacrificed? She'd been late but Pylia was innocent. She'd read somewhere that it was a bad omen if the sacrifice resisted. Well, she could tell them that this one was going to resist – and how! She looked at Pylia, but Pylia was staring transfixed at the floor in front of the screen. Penny couldn't see what she was looking at; the young priestess was in her way.

They stopped then before the old priestess and the girl moved aside. Penny and Pylia were each handed a beautifully carved stone pitcher with a long spout. There was liquid inside. Poison? Are we supposed to drink this and fall dead at the goddess's feet? She glanced over her shoulder. There was a gap behind her, and she was a good runner. She'd have surprise on her side. She could probably beat them back along the passage and maybe find the bull court and make her jump. It was worth a try.

CHAPTER ELEVEN

The liquid in the pitcher seemed innocent though, and no one had signalled her to drink – yet. In fact, it looked like milk. Again she glanced at Pylia who had moved forward and was beginning to kneel, still staring at the floor behind the old priestess.

When the priestess moved away Penny could see the pit in the floor that had been hidden by the screen. It was filled with snakes, writhing and twisting about.

Even someone like herself who loved snakes would be a bit nervous and Pylia was obviously scared stiff. Still she was bravely kneeling beside the pit. Then Penny realized what she was doing. There was a stone jar rather like the planter Penny's mother kept her parsley growing in. Little cups all around the sides. Pylia was trying to pour milk into one of the cups near the top but her hand was shaking so it looked as if she might spill. No doubt that would be a serious offense. On Penny's side of the pit there was a similar pot. She moved quickly. Maybe it would reassure Pylia if she did hers first and the snakes came to her side.

She knelt and filled the little cup at the top nearest the pit and was filling one a little lower down and to the front, when a huge snake rose from the centre of the nest.

The snake was twice as big as Monty. And Monty was a good-sized python, for a pet anyway, four or five feet long, maybe more. She and Katy had tried to stretch him out to measure him, but Monty hated being straightened out. This snake was as big around as her thigh and goodness knows how much of it there was still in the pit. It reared up to Penny, its tongue flicking in the lamplight.

It's only smelling for the milk, Penny told herself, and kept pouring as it came nearer.

She filled several more of the little cups as it drank from the one above. When she had emptied out her pitcher she looked over at Pylia and saw with relief that her friend had managed to fill the cups on her side as well. Now that the King snake had drunk, the smaller snakes swarmed out around the bottom cups. Penny watched Pylia so that they both rose together and backed away to their places in the circle. Only then did Pylia look at her and Penny could read the gratitude in her eyes.

There was a new tone now to the chanting. Evidently the goddess was pleased with their offering; even Medusa's face had softened a little. Penny could read relief in the way the girls stood, although they kept their respectful poses and silence.

They went back as quietly as they had come and once they were well under the palace, Pylia took her hand again and even smiled happily in the flickering light. She must have known it was her turn to make the offering even before we went, which was why she looked so hypnotized with fear once we got there, Penny thought. But she should be used to snakes; after all hadn't Mum said that every home had a house snake to keep the rats and mice away? Still Penny doubted that any of them reached the size of the monster in the cave, so she couldn't blame Pylia for being frightened.

Once they were alone in their little alcove, Pylia threw her arms around Penny and hugged her happily. Then she dug under her bed and pulled out some bunches of grapes. They sat cross-legged on their beds, eating and giggling companionably though Medusa had been by once already to scold them.

Although Pylia always spoke carefully to Penny to teach her the language, it was accompanied by sign language and they would point to each other and all around them. Sometimes the

communication took the form of hilarious charades that left them laughing and gasping for
breath. Like now, when Penny had asked what the
boys were doing while the girls were at the goddess rituals.

"They were," Pylia acted, "partying!" She guz-
zled on imaginary wine jugs, sang, danced, and
staggered about – generally indicating a pretty
wild time.

Penny laughed. For an athlete as dedicated as
Pylia was, she made a very convincing drunk.
Pylia also mimed throwing up and then drinking
some more.

It was now Penny's turn. "But what about the
bull? Tauros?" She played the bull coming in to
gore the drunken Pylia.

Pylia was serious now. "No bull tomorrow."
She shook her head. "The boys do not party when
there is a bull the next day." She waved her arms
to include the others and Penny understood what
she meant. "We would all die if they did."

That stopped the laughter, so that when
Medusa appeared suddenly – she had a way of
sneaking up on them – they were both silently
serious. Obviously the priestess was impressed and
she even gave them a nod and a slight relaxing of the
lips which, Penny thought, was probably as close as
she would ever come to a smile. She then smothered
the lamp in the alcove, although there was another
left on near the main doorway to the hall.

Penny lay in the dark listening to the sounds of the other girls settling down to sleep. Someone began to breathe loudly and, beside her, Pylia mumbled and sighed in her sleep. Was she dreaming of home? Penny wondered. She realized that she knew nothing of Pylia's background. Where had she come from? Was she tribute from some island that was subject to the Minoan power? Perhaps even, like Theseus, from Athens? But then Pylia didn't know about her background either. Perhaps the bull dancers, whose lives held no future but death, had to ignore the past as well. No past, no future, only the present.

Pylia had accepted Penny as her partner on the team. Rhion had not even seemed surprised that she was there. Obviously he thought she'd been sent as a replacement. For who? Pylia's former partner probably. She hadn't even thought of that. She didn't need to wonder what had happened to the girl whose place she was taking. She shuddered remembering the blood on the sand.

In silence at last, Penny got up and dressed in her own clothes and tiptoed out. She thought that she might have to deal with one of the priestesses, but they must have been sleeping too.

She had no difficulty finding her way again to the bull court, which was silent now in the moonlight. She staggered a bit and then caught her balance. Funny, it was almost as if the earth had somehow shuddered beneath her feet. But then

she often felt dizzy and she was probably just nervous – worried about getting back. She stood a
minute trying to calm herself, then bent to gather
a handful of sand to put in her pocket. She would
use it more carefully next time – if there was a
next time. She might not be so lucky another
time. And, she reminded herself, she wasn't back
yet.

Then, praying that she would not end up in
the bull court in the ruins of twenty-first century
Knossos, she began the flip.

CHAPTER TWELVE

Her feet slapped onto the marble floor of her hotel bedroom and she tumbled onto the bed.

"Good!" she thought. "So I end up wherever I started, even with the sand of the bull court." The clock on the stand said 3:30; she could still get some sleep. She took off her shorts, folded them carefully and placed them on the night table. She'd put them away in the morning.

Her mother got to them first.

Penny wakened from deep sleep to find bright sunshine streaming in the room and Mum standing there shaking the shorts out.

"Really Penny, how *do* you get so much sand in your pockets?" she complained. "Have you been rolling on the beach?"

Sand poured onto the floor and then there was a clinking sound and her mother bent over and retrieved something from under the bed.

"Mmmmph." Penny rolled over and shut her eyes. Maybe if she ignored her, Mum would go away and let her sleep.

No such luck. Mum was raving on about something else now. Penny opened one eye and then the other snapped open. Her mother was holding out the little golden bull.

"Where did you get this bull charm? It looks dreadfully expensive."

Penny made another "mmmmph" sound, hoping to buy some time. She could hardly say Dad had bought it – Mum would check that out before the words were out of her mouth. And she was right, it would be expensive. Penny had no doubt that it was pure gold. She looked at it gleaming orangey yellow in the sunlight as her mother held it towards her.

"Mmmmph...." more hesitation as if remembering, then, "...I got it the other day in that little shop near the Lion Fountain...when you were buying Dad those worry beads...." She let her voice trail off and started to roll over, then turned and held out her hand for the bull.

"Well my dear girl, you got a helluva bargain as your dad would say!"

Penny was relieved to feel the bull charm drop into her hand. She'd been afraid her mother would decide to show it to Dad and he would want to know how she'd been able to afford it.

"I'll look around for a nice gold charm bracelet for you to wear it on. It can be an early birthday present." Her mother was smiling down at her. "What a nice way to begin a travel charm bracelet...with a bull from Minos' palace!"

Penny smiled feebly. If you only knew Mum...if you only knew....

And she rolled over pretending to go back to sleep.

When the door closed behind her mother though, she was out of bed immediately. Carefully she used a dirty sock to sweep up the sand on the floor. She saved all she could, hiding it in an envelope in the writing-desk drawer. She'd better not have sand in her pockets again, or Mum would want to know why.

She was just brushing her teeth when her mother knocked on the door and held out a slender golden chain. "You can borrow this to keep your bull on so it doesn't get lost."

The chain just fit around Penny's neck so that the bull nestled in the hollow of her throat. Nice, she thought.

"Meet me downstairs for breakfast," Dad yelled as he pounded the door on his way by.

"Kalamari!" her mother said brightly as she sat down to the breakfast table.

"Good morning is *Kalimera*, dear." Her father pulled a woebegone clown face. "You've just called me a squid!"

Penny laughed. Her mother, for all her love of things Greek, was hopeless with languages. The only words she knew well were those connected with food. Penny had heard at least a hundred times the story about how she'd fallen for Dad because he took her to a Greek restaurant on their first date. Food was a big thing in this family. Tom could eat his way through a ham in no time. Why was it then, Penny wondered, that it just made her feel sick?

Remembering made her feel ill again. Any minute now her father would start nagging about eating. Mum wouldn't say anything, just watch Penny's plate like a hawk to see what was being eaten and what was only being pushed around.

The smell of Dad's overloaded plate was beginning to get to her. Eggs, potatoes, sausages, some strange fish, tiny fried dumplings like doughnut holes and some vegetable he claimed was eggplant. It was too much. Penny got up and headed for the buffet table just to get away.

There were some orange segments, like Christmas mandarins, that had a lovely sharp taste and she took some of the croissant-like pastry too. If she spread things around maybe her plate wouldn't appear too empty.

She tried but Dad couldn't resist a comment. "Is that all you could find? Eat up girl! Put a little meat on those bones!"

Penny's eyes filled with tears. She had enough

"meat on her bones." Too much. Or why else would Coach holler, whenever she flubbed a move: "Getting too tubby to do it? Gymnasts can't be overweight!" Sometimes he said it to some of the other girls, but mostly to her. And everyone would laugh, so she'd be bound to miss the jump or whatever after that. Anyway, the other girls didn't have a brother like Tom who had a series of nicknames for her – Tubby, Porkchop, Miss Piggy, and mostly ... Fatso. When he was on a roll he could use all of them in one sentence. When she was younger, if Mum and Dad were out so they were having supper alone, he wouldn't say anything at all, just sit there making pig noises at her as she tried to eat. That didn't happen now that she was older. Nowadays she didn't eat when Tom was around if she could help it.

Penny excused herself as soon as she could, went back to her room, locked herself in the bathroom and threw up.

Afterwards she lay on her bed holding the tiny bull at her throat until she fell asleep.

CHAPTER THIRTEEN

She woke, took a moment to remember where she was, then turned to see what time the clock said. But there was no clock – only Pylia's tousled head sleeping across from her.

Too much! Penny thought. Had she only dreamt the part of going back to the bull court, falling asleep at the hotel and having breakfast with Mum and Dad? Maybe she'd just fallen asleep here and dreamed the whole thing. It was possible. Something like that had happened to her before, when she was worried about an exam. She'd slept in, rushed around getting ready, been late for school, missed the exam and then found out she'd only dreamed it – the day and the exam were still ahead of her.

She'd been worried about getting back; maybe she'd dozed off waiting for the others to fall asleep. Now what would she do? It was daylight and she could hear voices in the room. Some of the other girls were awake. No doubt Medusa was lurking around keeping an eye on them. She'd just have to stay and see what happened.

Pylia sat up and looked across at her, smiling. No early morning grumps for her! Penny thought. Well I suppose if you only had a day left to live there'd be no point wasting it being cranky. That saying on the posters, "Today is the first day of the rest of your life" could be changed here to read "Today is the last day of the rest of your life." She got up and gave Pylia a hug and was startled when Pylia pointed, laughing, at her clothes. Penny was wearing her shorts and top. Not the ones she'd hidden under the mattress but the ones she'd put on this morning. So she hadn't dreamed her return. And since she hadn't thrown sand or done the beginning of the vault, what had done it? She remembered last thing before falling asleep rubbing the tiny bull around her neck. It must have brought her back when she slept. She'd have to be careful of that.

Pylia was still staring at her clothes, shaking her head. Then she smiled and began to apologize.

She thinks it's my native dress from wherever I was captured and brought here, I suppose. Penny smiled back. Well, I suppose it is – the traditional costume, summer costume that is, of the Canadian teenager!

Pylia had slipped into a loose tunic. While her back was turned Penny slipped hers over top of her own clothes. She'd have to find a place to hide them if they put on their practice kilt, but at least she had them in case they didn't come back here.

"So no bull today – what do we do?" she asked.

Pylia smiled, "We eat, we rest, we practise!" She mimed the actions to the words but Penny was beginning to understand.

"Boys too?" Penny asked straight out. No miming.

Pylia laughed. "Rhion too!" she teased.

Penny started to say something about Rhion and Charis but she was interrupted by a clapping of hands and Medusa's appearance. Those who were ready could come for breakfast.

A group of girls from another team started out. This time Medusa went ahead of them rapping on the massive wooden doors. Penny could hear metal scraping. At last the doors opened. So, it seems we're shut in from the outside. They really don't want us out partying, do they? She was lucky to have got away last night before the doors were closed and barred.

Medusa stayed behind. Apparently they could be trusted to find their way back. Penny was relieved to see they were going to the room where they had eaten before. It was close to the changing room and practice chamber, where she could find an opportunity to slip away to the bull court. She wondered whether, if she rubbed the tiny golden bull, it would take her back to the hotel from here. But she didn't want to disappear suddenly and frighten Pylia.

Besides, wonder of wonders, she was hungry. Nobody here seemed to think she was anything but the right size to be a bull dancer, though the bull dancers were all muscle, and slender as any ballet dancer. And bull dancers had to be strong – and to be strong you needed to eat. Penny followed Pylia, who was loading a platter for the two of them with orange segments and figs and other fruit she didn't recognize. They sat sharing the food. Penny was surprised how much of the talk around them she was able to understand. It made her feel grateful to her almost forgotten Yia-yia and the words they'd shared in those happy days.

Melanthro and Lukos seemed to be the only boys from the team who were there. Penny looked around but could see no signs of Rhion or the other four. She wondered if it would be all right to go over and ask about him. She began to figure out the words to use.

Then Pylia laughed and pointed. "There he is!"

Penny looked at her, startled. After all she hadn't said a word. But she followed Pylia's pointing finger and saw that Rhion had come in, yawning and looking a bit tousled. On him it looked good.

She looked up and smiled at him, happy to see he was coming this way. She'd deal with Pylia later. She'd seen the way her friend brightened whenever Melanthro came into the room.

But Rhion was cut short in his walk across the room. Charis ran up to him, grabbed his arm and pulled him over to a corner. She was obviously scolding him for something. Penny watched her attempt to smooth back the tightly curling hair, and turned away, pretending to concentrate on the fig she was eating though she'd suddenly lost her appetite. She couldn't wait to get to the bull court now.

"Do you want more food?" Pylia was asking.

Penny looked at her, confused. Her mind was on other things. She was wondering how much time had passed in the present while she'd been here – was it still morning back at the hotel? "Hmmm?" What had Pylia said?

Pylia was standing now with the empty platter, smiling at Penny's confusion. "More..." she said, pointing to the platter and to the tables of food, "...FOOD!"

Penny couldn't help but laugh. She shook her head.

"More...for ME!" Pylia joked, pointing to herself. Then she left for the table.

As soon as her back was turned Penny got up and made her way to the door. Sure that no one noticed her slip out, she began to head down the corridor to the bull court. She could see it ahead of her, bathed in sunshine. She began to walk faster.

There was the sound of running feet in the corridor behind her. Her impulse was to break into a run too, but she controlled herself and just kept walking as fast as she could.

"Penelope!"

It was Rhion's voice. She couldn't help but stop and turn. What did he want?

He ran up, smiling and speaking too quickly for her to understand. She stood confused.

"Come," he said, taking her arm gently. "We have to practise. We need you."

She didn't resist. How could she? She'd have no excuse not to come and besides, walking beside him like this was very nice. They didn't go to the usual practice room but to an open courtyard much smaller than the bull court. Three of the other boys were there and in the far corner tossing its head – a bull.

Penny started back, still held by Rhion. As she did so the bull began to move toward them. Not galloping or trotting or even walking – rolling! It was a very realistic bull, on wheels! Somebody must be inside or underneath propelling it along. Penny laughed in appreciation. And Rhion laughed with her, pleased at her delight. Then he let go of her and ran toward the bull.

The bull was life-sized with real bull horns

and hide. There was obviously a mechanism inside to move the head from side to side and to toss it up and down. Rhion reached the bull, seized the horns and did a handstand. The bull's head dropped forward and Rhion slipped to one side. He had not been running fast enough to clear the horns, now he clung to one as the bull tossed his head.

Pretend it's the bull court, Penny thought. If this happened with a real bull Rhion's life would be in serious danger. She ran forward trying to draw the bull's attention away, but whoever was guiding the bull knew how hard it was to change a real bull's focus. Only one thing would be in the bull's slow-witted mind – getting rid of this creature on his horn. And, Penny realized, the way to do it would be to lower his head and rub whatever or whoever it was off on the ground. Probably the person would be gored like that bull boy she'd seen before. Penny grabbed the other horn and yanked with all her strength. It didn't have much effect, just as it probably wouldn't have with a real bull. But suddenly a voice very unlike the bellow of a bull came from inside, a trap door opened and out tumbled Alektryon. That's where the missing member of the team was, Penny thought, surprised. She should have guessed.

"Penelope! You must confuse the bull, not pull his head off!" Alektryon called. "You nearly broke Daedalus!" He laughed as the others joined in.

Penny laughed too. Daedalus? Was this where the myth came from? The famous bull Daedalus was supposed to have built for Pasiphae, Minos' queen, to hide in was the bull dancers' practice bull? She stood shaking her head in disbelief.

Rhion was the first to sober up. As usual there was a lesson to be learned in practice. One of them – maybe even both – would have been killed had it been a real bull.

He came over to her. "Sometimes you can survive one mistake in the court, but not two. Usually two mistakes and someone dies. Mine was the first mistake, for my stand on the horns to work there must movement...mine or the bull's. I was slow. The bull," he waved at Alektryon and raised his voice, "...the bull...was *very* slow!"

The others laughed again but Rhion was speaking seriously now for only Penny to hear.

"And you, my very brave Penelope," he paused, looked at her thoughtfully and gently touched her cheek, "very brave...very beautiful Penelope...you made a mistake too. You take a chance to save someone...someone on the team...but be sure you can clear yourself away if the bull turns on you."

And he led her to the bull and made her practise getting herself out of the way of the bull's horns.

The rest of the girls came in then and were taking turns with the bull. Rhion seemed to be everywhere, guiding and instructing. Penny stood at the edge of the little courtyard and watched. Then she slipped away.

This time, alone in the darkened corridor she did not head for the bull court. She merely held the tiny golden bull, rubbing it between her fingers until she remembered no more.

CHAPTER FOURTEEN

She woke up to feel her mother shaking her. "Are you all right, Penny?" As usual her mother's voice was concerned, "I thought you disappeared suddenly at breakfast. It's nearly ten o'clock...your father is rarin' to get started...he wants to drive to Agios Nicolaos for lunch."

Lunch! Penny moaned at the thought of another meal. It was only ten o'clock, so she'd been sleeping less than half an hour. She groaned again and started to bury her face in the pillow, then changed her mind. She didn't want her mother to think she was really sick.

"Why don't you guys go without me?" At first the idea was just like saying "go away and leave me alone" only more politely, but then as the sleep cleared from Penny's mind, it seemed like not a bad idea at all. "I could lie by the pool...I haven't had a chance to sunbathe...or read...." She sat up trying to look healthy but just a mite tired from all the sightseeing they'd been doing. "Please, Mum!"

"Poor Penny..." her mother looked sympathetic, "...well, it *is* supposed to be a holiday...." She seemed to be talking to herself now. "Just because your father's idea of one is to cover every inch of the island, doesn't mean that should be yours." She got up. "I'll talk to him."

Penny smiled and snuggled back down. Mum was in a convincing mood; Dad would surely have to give in. She lay there waiting. She really wasn't sleepy or tired now, but she'd stay here looking lazy until her mother got back. Wouldn't it be wonderful to have a day to herself!

Her mother came back. "Your father says 'do not go wandering around the streets,' 'stay around the hotel,' and..." she placed a five-thousand drachma note on the table, "Eat Lunch!"

"Yes, Mum," Penny smiled and waved a lazy hand from the pillow. "Have fun!"

She gave them twenty minutes to be safely gone, then got up. Good thing she'd been under the covers. She was still wearing the tunic thing she'd put on when she and Pylia dressed. She stuffed it under her pillow – it *was* sort of like a shortie nightgown – and put on her bikini. She'd lie by the pool for awhile. In the hot morning sun of Crete she was sure it wouldn't take long to get a little tinge of sunburn, enough to be convincing that she'd done what she'd said she would do.

She was right. By eleven o'clock she was back in the room rubbing lotion on her shoulders and neck. Her plan was to go back to bed, touch the bull and see what happened. She stood in front of the mirror looking at it nestled against her throat. Rhion's present.

She slipped on the tunic and lay on her bed. The sun had made her drowsy. If she slept would she be back in the locked-in alcove with Pylia? She fingered the tiny golden bull.

She was in the corridor again. The one from the practice court that she'd left. That seemed to be the way the bull worked. Was everyone still out in the practice ring? She'd noticed that the girls had been in their bull dancer's kit. Before she went back she'd go and change.

Anyway it was cool and dark in the corridor. Quiet. Out there in the practice ring Rhion had said "my brave, beautiful Penelope." Thinking about it made her happy. At first. Then she felt anger. *"My* Penelope?" What about *"My* Charis?" I'm jealous, she thought. That's wrong. Charis hasn't done anything to me. And it's wrong of Rhion to make a rivalry. Wrong and very dangerous. He's captain of a life-and-death team.

After the bull boy had died, the one she'd seen gored in the ring, Pylia had said something about a teammate setting him up. Maybe not that, but not making an effort to be there for him. She hadn't understood as much of the language then. It might not have been a jealousy over a person, maybe just a rivalry to be the best. The bull dancers had fans; she'd seen them receive gifts. And she knew people bet on performances each time they danced. Even bet on whether a certain daring bull boy or girl would survive to dance another day.

Maybe he likes us both, but I'll have to be careful, she decided. Careful in the ring. Now she didn't have to worry only about the bull, but about Charis too. Maybe she should talk to Pylia. After all, Pylia had known them longest.

She had a whole day before they danced for the bull again.

She'd barely finished changing before the others came in tired and sweating from practice in the hot sun. Some went and stood in the tiny alcoves Penny'd noticed before. Servants came in with large pitchers of water to pour over them, the water sluicing away down some of the tour guide's famous drains. They didn't dry themselves then but took turns with a sort of scraper removing the sweat and dust. Pylia came over, her dark skin glowing.

"Time to eat!" she said merrily. "What I do best!"

Maybe it was, Penny thought as she fell into step beside her, but it doesn't show.

"You two," said Melanthro as they passed by

him, "are like two perfect little dolls – just the same! One dark, one light."

Pylia only laughed but Penny caught the look that passed between them. Penny didn't care; she wanted to thank him. She knew her skin was paler even though her hair was dark and curly – what her mother called her "Greek look" – but if Melanthro thought she was just like Pylia physically, that was a great compliment. There wasn't an ounce of fat on Pylia, just the perfectly toned muscle of an athlete. And that was how Penny wanted to be.

She did not go back that night. If minutes were hours in the past, she decided, a day would give her plenty of time. She practised with the others, ate, rested and talked to Pylia. She could understand now although Pylia laughed at her mixed-up words sometimes. Mostly they communicated very well. They still acted the charades for fun, though, imitating Medusa or some of the others. But they hadn't talked about Rhion. Somehow Penny hadn't wanted to. She'd ignored him at suppertime, though she'd seen him looking at her more than once and known that if she'd smiled he'd have come over. But she always looked away. Pretending great interest in her food or something Pylia was saying.

This was the longest she'd ever been here but she did not see much more of the palace complex than she had already seen. Obviously the bull dancers, though treated well, were little more than prisoners, especially the girls.

It would have been nice, she thought, lying on the narrow bed that night, to have been able to explore. To go to the queen's Megaron and see the dolphins as they had originally been, and the blue and red pillars or the great haut relief mural of the charging bull. She'd been rather pleased that she'd remembered about "haut reliefs" being raised carvings in a wall mural, where the figures were not only carved but stood out like sculpture. And she would have liked to see one of those famous flush toilets. What they used was a place where the drain was open with running water underneath. Sort of natural flushing, but not the ones that had caused such amazement when they were discovered. Amazing all right. An invention that had to be reinvented over three thousand years later!

She'd had glimpses of the pillars when they were in the bull court but then you weren't looking at much but the bull. No time to sightsee. If she remembered correctly the bull mural was visible from the central court in Evans' reconstructed bit of the palace. Maybe tomorrow when they took their bows she would look for it. Tomorrow they would dance for the bull again.

She touched the bull at her throat and slept.

CHAPTER FIFTEEN

She'd changed back into her bikini just before she fell asleep, so that if she didn't wake up before Mum and Dad got back it would be all right. Lucky though, that she did. She lay there thinking about going back down to the pool and getting into sunbathing mode and was getting up to do it when she noticed the lunch money still on the table where Mum had left it. It would have been the first thing Mum saw if she'd walked in while Penny was sleeping. Quickly she slipped it into her purse and left some crumpled bills and a few coins. Change from lunch.

She made it to the pool and had managed to put lotion on all the parts she could reach before they got back.

"There you are Penny!" Her mother was standing there looking down at her, smiling but tired. "Your dad and I are just going to have a drink over there at the bar." She waved to the poolside umbrella tables where Dad was already sitting and turned to leave. "I see you had lunch. Good girl."

Penny's stomach did a little flip of gratitude. Mum had checked and the change had told the story. She hadn't even been given the third degree as to what she'd eaten. Now all she had to do was get through the rest of the day and supper before she could go back. She didn't even stop to analyze why she wanted so much to go back. She did. It's because of Pylia, she told herself. We're a team, the two of us.

But it wasn't Pylia that Rhion chose to go with Penny and him the next day at noon when the bull dance started. It was Charis.

Penny had noticed before that a few team members sometimes watched the teams who were in the ring earlier, as they had the day she'd seen the youth killed. It was, she supposed, what the teachers at home would have called a learning experience.

So there they sat, close to the entrance they would later be coming through. It gave her a chance to look around – to see the wooden stands, like bleachers at a ball game but more elegant. Though their seats were nothing compared to the canopied boxes at the end. That must be where the royal family sat. The king. Minos. The tour guide had said that Minos was really a title, like Tsar or King, not the name of one person. Penny wondered. She had heard the name referred to, but her command of the language was too poor to get into political discussions. It didn't seem to matter much to the bull dancers – they had other things on their minds. There was no one in the boxes now. But the stands were filling with richly dressed people. Not like Romans in great togas and cloaks, the men were bare to the waist, bare that is except for the jewelled golden collars. The women wore tops with sleeves that covered their shoulders and arms, but left their breasts bared – either with a neckline that plunged to the waist or gathered beneath the breasts the way the priestesses' were. The women were even more heavily adorned with jewels than the men – golden bracelets and rings gleamed in the sun.

Penny was too interested in looking around to pay much attention to Rhion sitting between the two girls, but Charis was pointing to something now – a young woman, princess or priestess, had suddenly appeared in what Penny thought of as the Royal box.

And now, to Penny's surprise, Charis slipped away from her place on the bench beside Rhion and came to sit on Penny's other side.

"The daughter of Minos is here today," she said quietly to Penny as everyone stood. There was no cheering. Soon they sat again. "She is also the greatest priestess. An oracle of Mother Dia."

Penny had the impression of a tiny woman, not much more than a child. Her face was heavily painted, especially her eyes. Even from here her lowered eyelids glittered as though sprinkled with gold dust. Maybe they're too heavy for her to open properly, Penny thought. Now she had disappeared behind a thin curtain that dropped in front of her as she sat under a canopy.

"The curtain protects her from the sun and dust," Charis smiled at Penny, "...probably from the smell of the people too." She laughed.

She is being so nice, Penny thought. Not jealous of me or a bit mean-spirited. She tried to smile back, feeling a bit ashamed of herself. Was Charis being so nice because she didn't think Penny was a threat? Or was there something else? Penny was relieved when the first team of bull dancers entered. They ran to the far end of the court, formed a backward V with the captain in the front. There was no time to think of anything else. The music changed and rose – there had been music all along, Penny realized, surprised that she hadn't noticed it. The bull entered from the corridor close beneath them. All her focus would be on him now. She held her breath as the captain gave the salute, moved slowly forward and stood waiting.

The bull stood too. It was the black one who'd killed the boy the first day he'd been in the ring. He seemed more used to the bull court now.

Calmer. She looked down at him. A huge bull, bigger even than the Charolais bulls she'd seen when Dad took her to the Agricom at the Ex when she was a kid. Far bigger than the small black fighting bulls of Spain she'd seen in bullfight movies. She wanted to ask Rhion about that, but what would he know of a sport that came millennia after his own time? The bull was still standing where he had entered, looking around as if wondering whether he should be bothered today.

Rhion leaned toward her. "To be chosen as an offering to Poseidon, a sacred bull for the bull court, the bull must be perfect in size, with large horns that have no flaw." Penny looked at the gilded horns and hooves. Somebody must paint them. The bull's hide gleamed in the sunshine. Somebody must groom it the way she'd seen people groom prize bulls for the show.

"He seems to be very tame..." she whispered and then realized how silly that sounded. This bull was a killer – she'd seen it herself.

"That is the most dangerous. His brain is slow. He is wondering what to do. So far he has not decided whether he is threatened or not. He can smell us and the others in the stands, and he has not figured out that it is only the team at the far end that he can reach."

The crowd was starting to grumble, growing impatient. There was a nasty rumble of sound, like booing from a modern crowd.

"The captain must move...must coax the bull out into the ring so that the team can begin the dance."

But the captain was not moving and the sound of the crowd became ugly and threatening. The music had risen too. Shrieking and ferocious – a discordant sound that made Penny cringe.

Rhion's voice was desperate. "He's lost his nerve." He shook his head sadly.

Penny remembered that day in the bullring when Rhion bravely lured the bull into the centre of the court so that the team could perform, could "dance the bull."

On the other side of her, Charis's voice was hushed. "If you lose your nerve in the ring, you die."

Still neither the bull nor the captain of the team moved. The others stood obediently as if awaiting his lead and the sound of the crowd grew even more ominous. People were throwing things.

Finally, one of the other boys on the team moved forward past the captain and ran towards the bull, saluting it. The charge was swift. Too swift, Penny thought. He can't get out of the way and he won't have time to take the bull's horns and leap. But he did. He flew through the air, pro-pelled by the momentum of the charge and quick enough to let go of the horns. There was no one to catch him and he landed sprawled on the ground.

But the bull did not slow its charge. Not far in front of him the captain still stood and he was its focus. The rest of the team scattered, taking positions encircling the bull. When the bull was almost on him, the youth moved at last, but the bull was ready to gore now and turned its head, so that though he tried to grasp the horns, one slipped away. He was holding to one horn, the way Rhion had been with the practice bull when Penny'd rushed in to grab the other. This time nobody rushed in to grab the other horn.

At first the bull dragged the unfortunate captain along the ground, then finally, with a mighty twist of its head, shook him loose. He tried to crawl away, bleeding from being dragged, but the bull was too quick.

Penny couldn't stand it. She grabbed Rhion's arm. "Somebody should help him!" she moaned. But none of the team would come that close. And now the bull was tossing him in the air. Like a rag doll. There was blood everywhere. She buried her face in Rhion's shoulder. "Somebody should have..." she sobbed.

He had his arm around her, "...helped him?" he murmured softly. "Like you did for me? Like I would do for you?"

Penny looked at him. She did not want to look into the ring below. Rhion was shaking his head.

"They would not. They are afraid of him now.

When a captain loses his nerve he endangers the team. Nothing can save him. He has met his bull."

Penny looked down. The bull was gone, the dancers were gone, it was over. Charis was standing, her face tightly drawn. She took Penny's hand.

"It's all right," she said softly. "It was their captain, not ours."

Penny followed her miserably. She was aware of Rhion walking behind them. How could she go in with the team when their turn came to face the bull? What if she lost her nerve? It wasn't just her own life, she realized that now. It was other lives as well. Pylia's. And Rhion's.

In the darkness of the corridor she felt her fingers move toward the little golden bull at her throat.

CHAPTER SIXTEEN

She could leave. Go back. She would be safe in her bed at the hotel. Safe. Away from the blood and fear and death. And her team would be one short. They'd manage – Pylia would be without a partner. But it would be better than having a partner who was afraid.

She didn't dare touch the bull yet. Charis still held her hand – Rhion walked just behind. It would be too shocking for them to have her disappear. In a few minutes they had to dance the bull. They'd think it was some terrible omen of the gods or something. Rhion might lose *his* nerve, might stand like the doomed captain of the other team until it was too late. Penny's hand dropped from where it had lingered at her throat. What if she slipped away and did it where no one could see? They would think she'd chickened out and abandoned them – that might be unnerving too. She did care.

She knew how much when she saw Pylia run towards her, her face all sympathy, her arms out to hug. She knew how much when she saw Rhion look at her before he began his usual talk to the team, what she'd thought of once as his "pre-game pep talk."

"This team," Rhion began, "This team has survived longer than any other in the bull court because we care about each other." He was looking at each one in turn. "Just now we saw a captain die – a team lose pride. You must know that you can count on me – and on each other – or we are not a team but individuals. Brave individuals who will die one by one – alone in the bull court."

Penny gazed at him. He's a born leader, she thought. I wonder what his destiny would have been had he not been brought to dance and die in the bull court? She was so caught up by his voice that she stopped listening to the words. One thing she knew, she would not lose her nerve today.

"We are not alone," Rhion finished. "We have each other!"

Spontaneously, they began to hug, or clasp arms. When it was Rhion's turn to hug her she could only smile. Last she and Pylia hugged. But when Penny looked over Pylia's shoulder she saw who Rhion's last, longest hug was for – Charis. And once again, in spite of herself, she felt the tinge of resentment towards her.

Penny tried not to think of it as they entered the bullring. They moved gracefully across the court and formed their V. The music played, the crowd cheered, for the Dolphins were a favoured team. If it weren't for the bloodstains on the freshly raked sand, Penny thought, we might be an Olympic team entering the stadium on opening day. If it weren't for the bloodstains – and the waiting bull.

Her mind was racing. She wanted this to be over, not because she'd lost her nerve now, but because she wanted to think. If only she could be an Ariadne with the *clew* to help Rhion escape. But she knew no bull dancer had ever escaped. She and Pylia had talked about it. It was said that if a dancer survived for two years in the ring he or she would be given freedom. Pylia didn't know if this was true or just a tale. No bull dancer had survived for even a year. The Dolphins, at least the core of the team – Rhion, Melanthro, Lukos and Charis – had been together for nearly six months. Pylia and Alektryon were the most recent to become part of it, except for Penny.

Penny shook her head. She must stop this and concentrate. The bull would be entering soon. Where was it? They'd been standing here longer than they should. The crowd was getting restless as they had before, although this time nobody could blame Rhion. This was bad. It put the wrong tension on them and would undo Rhion's pep talk. She could see him standing, waiting to salute the bull – his shoulders tense.

There was murmuring now. A rumour circulating that the black bull had been difficult after leaving the court, so he was still in the pen and their bull could not be brought in. At least the crowd's restlessness abated a little. More rumours. Penny looked across at Pylia. They were closest to the stands and could hear most, for they stood at each end of the widest part of the V – the Dolphins had not broken rank. Now there was talk that the black bull had killed one of the men who handled it – maybe two. She wondered how much of this, if any, Rhion could hear, or whether he still waited not knowing.

For the first time Penny actually wished the bull would come. The wait was too much – somebody, everybody would lose nerve, make mistakes. But Pylia caught her eye and smiled and Penny took a deep breath. They were a team. She was a Dolphin.

And then there he was. The bull. But it was not their bull. Not the white bull they'd danced for every time before. It was the black bull. And both horns were bloodstained now.

There was an excited murmur that became a roar of talk – she could hear bets being exchanged – bets that a Dolphin would die today. And then the bull charged.

Large though he was, he could move. And he

came towards them where they stood set up like bowling pins, with Rhion the kingpin, still standing with his arm raised in salute.

Someone, Penny thought later it was Charis, yelled then. "Move!" And as one they did. Leaping forward, Penny and Pylia, the furthest in the rear, had time for somersaults as if this were an ordinary bull they were dancing for. The others leaped and turned, coming up beside Rhion.

Penny landed, watching the bull. Rhion had not moved but the charge had slowed. All the movement was working – confusing the bull. She held her breath. Had Rhion lost his nerve like the other captain? No. As the bull neared he ran forward, seized the horns quickly, did a perfect handstand and flipped over before the bull had time to toss his head or turn it aside. Somehow Melanthro and Alektryon were in position to catch him and Lukos was there in front, Charis beside him, to hold the bull's attention.

Before the bull could change direction, Lukos ran forward, again grabbed the horns and flipped. That was it – the way the team should go. One after another. Leaping the bull. Penny felt a thrill of exultation. They would do it! The bull had stopped and merely snorted and pawed the ground now – confused. Now they could run at him, like a practice bull except for having to worry about him twisting his head at the wrong moment.

Charis was next. But as she ran, she slipped

and fell. She'd been right in front, ready to follow Lukos. Later they thought she might have slipped in the blood under the sand. No one knew. But as she struggled to get up, the bull lowered his head and began to move again.

Penny could see Rhion running from behind the bull, on his face a look of terrible fear and pain. There was nobody near enough. Nobody but Penny.

"Get her away!" she screamed. She darted forward and seized the bull by the horns. His head was lowered to gore, too low for her to do a proper handstand and flip. But she was small and quick. She swung her feet over the top of his head, pushing them between the horns and jumped. She didn't go far. She landed, legs astride the bull's back. Facing tailwards – more like some demented rodeo clown than a graceful bull dancer.

And there she sat. Afraid to slip to one side or the other in case the bull turned – and she couldn't see what he was doing. She could see the shocked look on Melanthro's face. Never having seen this move before, he gave her no signal of what to do. She fully expected the bull to madly buck her off, but this was no rodeo Brahma. The bull wasn't moving.

Her heart sank. Did that mean he was preparing to gore? Who? Charis? Or Rhion?

Melanthro had run up alongside now and

held up his hands. She gratefully seized them, letting him flip her ungracefully over, though she made a gymnast's recovery of a bad landing and a sloppy bow.

Was it her imagination or was the crowd silent? Sometimes they were, at a death. She didn't want to look to the front of the bull and see what had happened, so she faced the crowd instead.

But they weren't silent at all. They cheered, some of them on their feet. She looked to the front of the bull expecting to see a crumpled body beneath his head. But there was none. The team was moving behind the barrier, leaving the court. Melanthro grabbed her hand and pulled her along, shutting the gate behind them.

CHAPTER SEVENTEEN

Rhion was waiting for her in the corridor. "Thank you!" was all he said, but he held her a long time.

Then it was Charis's turn. Penny hadn't noticed her standing by, wasn't ready for her hug.

"Thank you!" she said, "Thank you, Sister!"

It would have been rude to break away from Charis's hug but Penny nearly did....

Sister? Charis was way ahead of her time! Or maybe the trend Penny'd noticed in women of her mother's generation was just a revival of something very old? Or maybe...? Another thought struck her and she was glad that the others had moved on to the changing chamber and couldn't see her face.

Maybe – the thought stopped her in her tracks – maybe the ancient Minoans had believed in multiple marriages. Maybe she and Charis were the beginning of some kind of future harem of Rhion's, and Charis just naturally accepted Penny into the "family." The thought made her angry and a little sick.

She was far enough behind now – she grabbed the bull at her throat.

Penny woke up wondering why she felt so ill at ease. Then she remembered she'd come back upset by Charis calling her sister. Now in the bright morning light, she almost laughed. Such a stupid idea! Rhion's future harem. Ridiculous! But it wasn't funny – the improbable idea of the future harem – the idea of bull dancers *having* a future.

Once again Penny wracked her brain for a way to escape the palace – the House of the Axe – the Labyrinth. But she knew more about it from the tour of the ruins than from living there. The queen's Megaron, the throne room, the corridor of the procession – for all the bull dancers knew, those parts of the Palace might not have existed.

Could she use the little golden bull somehow to put herself in other parts of the palace? Even if she could, she could hardly overpower guards and help her friends escape. And now she would not want to help only Pylia and Rhion to freedom. What about Charis? Rhion would never leave without her. What about Melanthro and the others – her team, the Dolphins? If she could help some escape, how could she leave the others to die?

She thought of what might happen after an

escape. Where would they go? Crete was the largest of the Aegean islands, three or four times bigger than any of the others. She'd seen how rugged the mountain areas were. They'd driven for what seemed like hours without seeing signs of people. And hadn't Dad gone on about how hundreds of British and New Zealand soldiers had hidden out in the mountains for nearly a year after Crete fell to the Germans in World War II? Her teammates were resourceful, they'd manage. No, the big thing – the impossible thing – would be getting them out of the Palace.

It was true that the longer you lived in the bull court, the better you were at the movements that helped you survive, the better at second-guessing the movements of the bull. Pylia had told her that and she'd seen it herself. But some day there would be one mistake too many. One of the team would "meet his bull" or "her bull," as the saying went. Then no matter how eloquent Rhion's pep talks were, the team would start to fear. And die.

"You're very quiet, Penny?" her mother said at breakfast.

"Let her be," her dad responded. "At least she's eaten a good breakfast for once."

Penny looked down at her plate. To her surprise it seemed she had eaten most of what had been there. There were traces of omelette and part of a slice of bacon but it really looked as though there'd been food there. She couldn't remember eating it but she felt comfortably full. A strange feeling – usually when she forced food down she felt sick and couldn't wait to get to the bathroom.

"I was afraid perhaps you weren't feeling well."

Penny looked startled. That coming from Mum! Now she was sick if she didn't eat and sick if she ate! Talk about a no win situation. She tried not to sound annoyed.

"No Mum, I'm fine." She wanted to leave, but then Mum would be on again about her being sick. "I'll just get another glass of juice – does anyone else want one?"

Maybe, she hoped, they'll leave, and I can have another day by the pool. Too much to hope for, she thought glumly. But the breakfast must have brought her luck; when she got back there seemed to be a heated discussion – and this time Dad was on her side.

"We're going to the Monastery of Arkadh this morning," her mother spoke first. "Your father thinks you might rather stay here and enjoy another sunny day by the pool." The implication in her mother's voice was that this was too ridiculous to credit.

Nice try, Mum, Penny thought. "That's the one where everybody got blown up during the War of Independence from the Turks?" Penny said. She was gratified to see their surprised looks – but what else did they expect? She'd spent hours sitting in the back seat with the guidebook as they'd criss-crossed Crete. So, now they were impressed. Time to cash in on it. She looked at her father knowing where her ally was. "It really would be nice to stay. I've seen quite a few monasteries..." She let her voice trail off.

Was it ten they'd been to? It seemed like dozens. She didn't want to say: "if you've seen one Byzantine monastery, you've seen them all," because she had to admit it wasn't true. For instance there was that lovely little one just north of Kolimbari right on the water with the won-derful view of the Aegean Sea and the White Mountains from the little balcony. All of them were perched on hilltops or cliffsides with incred-ible views. She had to admit those early monks knew how to pick a building site.

Penny tried not to look at her mother. She didn't want to see the disappointed look.

"That settles it then, we're off!" Dad was picking up his camera and the eternal guidebook. He studied it religiously and from time to time would come up with some little-known fact. Like now, "Did you know," he said, giving Penny a hug and slipping her a bill, "that there are thirteen million olive trees in Crete?"

"And I've seen them all!" her mother mum-bled under her breath.

Penny was sure Dad hadn't heard, but now she understood why Mum had wanted her to go – she would rather be suntanning by the pool herself!

Penny watched them go, then looked down at the bill in her hand. Another five thousand drachmas. She'd been very impressed by the spending money Dad had given her when they'd first arrived – until she'd learned that a coke was two hundred (or two hundred fifty depending on the mood of the salesman in the kiosk you went to) and just about any souvenir would be two or three thousand. Her father's adored *Guide to Crete* had set him back seven thousand or so.

She went back to her room, changed into her bikini, grabbed the Knossos guidebook with its detailed map of the palace and headed for the pool. She had a lot of planning to do. It *was* like a maze. First she tried to figure out where their quarters were. Easy to find the central court so the entry at the north end must be it. So how did you get out? The trouble was that the palace had so many levels. What level was represented by this map? Evans had rebuilt in a few places showing several storeys but otherwise the ruins had collapsed on themselves. It might be easy to draw a line finding her way out on this map – she felt like she was doing one of those little kid maze puzzles – but it was another matter with the real thing. Even with Ariadne's ball of string it would be hard to do. And after all, Ariadne, whether she was real or just a character in a myth, had been the king's daughter in her own palace and would have a better chance of finding her way around.

She thought of smuggling the map back and discussing it with Pylia but she gave up the idea. Even if she could get around explaining that this was a map from the future, she really didn't think it would be of much use.

She started over. She had managed to get into the bull court a couple of times when she'd been using that route back to the present. Nobody'd seen her, or at least they hadn't cared. A bull dancer doing a leap in the bull court might not be questioned. What if she crossed the full length of the courtyard? According to the map of the ruins this would bring her to the famous Corridor of the Procession – named for the frescoes of a procession bearing gifts to the king – and from there to the west court where people entered the ruins today. No, better to take the other corridor to the southwest porch. And down the steps. But it was a long way. And it would have to be done in the daytime since they were locked in at night.

"How very admirable to see a young lady studying on her holiday!" The voice came from right behind her.

Penny jumped, nervously. She almost felt as if she'd been caught in her getaway attempt already. Then she caught herself and smiled up at the guest who'd spoken, mumbled, "thank you," and turned the page as if reading more about the palace. She hoped the lady would take the hint and move on. But she took a chair near Penny and looked as if she might want to continue the conversation. Penny looked at her watch and jumped up, mumbling about being late and hurried off to her room.

She lay down on the bed and touched the bull once more.

CHAPTER EIGHTEEN

When she entered the changing chamber it was deserted. What time was it? Had she been gone a long time? In here it was hard to tell because there was no skylight and the room was always dark except for the oil lamps. To her relief she could hear voices. They would be in the chamber beyond – eating, perhaps, or resting. Maybe if she slipped in quietly they wouldn't notice she had disappeared.

But when she entered the talk stopped. Everyone stared at her. Now what? thought Penny. She smiled ruefully. Probably it was her embarrassing backward bull ride they were remembering. Pylia came towards her laughing and pointing to the bikini. Penny'd forgotten to change again. Well they might laugh, but they'd just put it down to another eccentric native costume – she hoped. She'd learned that no one questioned where you came from or how you'd got here. It seemed to be some sort of bull dancers' code. The past was gone and reliving it might be painful and could do no good. For a bull dancer there was only now.

Pylia came as close as anyone when she teased Penny about her clothes. "You are a brazen one Penelope – you cover your breasts and allow your shoulders to be seen!"

Penny realized that she had never seen any of the women with bared shoulders – except the bull girls of course, and they wore the same clothes as the boys but only in the ring. In the bull court they needed freedom to move. Nothing to catch on the bull's horns. Their jewellery always had a weak link so that if it caught it could easily break and pull free. But they were not in the bullring now and Penny suddenly felt very naked – embarrassed by her bare shoulders.

They walked back to the changing room together to find Penny something "decent" to put on.

Pylia was chattering on about what had happened in the ring. "...And now Rhion wants us...those of us who are short...small enough to do it, anyway...to learn to do that move you did today. The way you did the kind of handstand and slipped your legs between your arms so quickly...so you must teach me. It is a good thing to do when the bull's head is down too low for a proper handstand."

Penny laughed. "And does he want me to teach you to ride the bull backwards too?"

"No," Pylia giggled. "He didn't say that but he wants Melanthro and the others to practise catching 'those who land strangely' on the back of the bull!"

Later, as they lounged on cushions on the stone benches, eating with the others, Penny absently watched a servant enter and begin lighting some of the oil lamps in the room.

Pylia looked up. "It's getting dark," she said.

Startled Penny stared up too. Why had she not paid attention to the fact that there was a sky-light here? And because there was no glass in ancient Crete, it was open. True it was covered by the room above like the one in the reconstructed king's Megaron she'd seen on the tour – another place for the tour guide to rave about the drains – but there would be access to the room above.

"Pylia," she whispered urgently. "What's above us?"

She thought she'd been very quiet but Rhion had been standing not far away. Now he came and sat beside Penny.

He glanced up then stared at the floor. "It is open and the room is empty. And I have heard that it leads to the roof of the palace further on." He spoke softly for the servant had not left the room, though the voices of the others would have drowned him out, Penny was sure.

"Then why... ?" She began, keeping her eyes on the pomegranate she was eating as if her primary concern was removing each juicy seed successfully.

"Why...?" Rhion said softly. "...why has no bull dancer ever stood on another's shoulders and gone through?" He paused, glanced quietly around the room at the departing servant, and bit into a fig.

Penny wanted to shake him. "Yes, why...?" she said impatiently, raising her voice a little.

When he spoke again it was even more softly and his voice was sad. "They have."

She couldn't bear it. "But Pylia said that no one had ever escaped these quarters."

Rhion sighed, "Perhaps she should have said... and lived!" He looked at Penny now and smiled sadly, took pity on her impatience and explained. "It was when I first came here. There were two dancers, boy and girl, they were lovers and so they wanted to live.... They did not."

It was Penny's turn for sorrow. She asked no more questions.

"Some say there would be no escape anyway. Bull dancers are dedicated to the god," Rhion spoke softly. "Some say they would have incurred the wrath of Poseidon for having cheated his bull," he shrugged hopelessly. "Perhaps even had they left the Palace and found a place to hide they would not have been able to hide from the vengeance of the god."

Penny shuddered. "Would *you* go if you could?"

Rhion thought a while. "We should not torture ourselves with these ideas." He shook his head sadly. "There is no point thinking of things that cannot be. When there is no choice, it is not wise to choose." Then he looked at her and tried to smile as he got up to go. "We have a saying Penelope – it is in the hands of the gods."

Penny watched him leave. It hurt to see the slump of his shoulders and know that she had caused him distress by insisting on talking of things that hurt.

But she couldn't give up. There had to be a way. We've got a saying about our God too, Rhion, she thought: God helps those who help themselves.

Casually she walked over to the other side of the low stone table spread with food. Even though there was plenty on her side, as she bent to pick up another pomegranate she looked up – through the skylight – into the gathering darkness above. She could see nothing to indicate the nature of the room or the roof above. Then, deep in thought, she returned to sit down beside Pylia.

A thought struck her. "Why can't the boys escape? They're not locked up at night as we are...they get to party." She leaned forward offering Pylia some of the seeds.

Pylia smiled at her, shaking her head. "But they can never leave the palace unless they are escorted to a special house. And they are watched very closely." She looked down at the fruit and said softly. "I think it's been tried...unsuccessfully," and her voice trailed off. She poked Penny and nodded to the doorway. Medusa had entered and stood impatiently waiting.

One by one the girls left their places and lined up quietly. Some hid pieces of fruit or sweetmeats in their sleeves to eat later. Pylia took her hand and Penny felt the sticky figs she had palmed and had to hold a laugh.

But as they walked she began to think again. Like a dog worrying a bone, her mind clung to the idea of escape. Rhion had not said he wouldn't go. Only that it was impossible. Maybe it wasn't. But she was disheartened by the knowledge that the boys were almost as much prisoners as they were, though it relieved her mind a little to believe that perhaps not all of them stayed out of fear of the god Poseidon.

At present she was sure only of Pylia. Though it hadn't been said in so many words she was sure Pylia did not feel any obligation to the god. And if she could save one person from death, especially someone as nice as Pylia, it would be worthwhile.

CHAPTER NINETEEN

enny continued to try to devise an escape plan. She'd thought the girls were more imprisoned than the boys. Now she knew it wasn't true. The girls actually left the palace when they went to the shrine. That gave her a twinge of hope. She remembered that brief time when they'd moved out of the passageway into the moonlight before entering the cave. Was there a pathway – a way down the hillside? She hadn't looked, she'd been too focused on following those ahead of her.

She could hardly contain her excitement, couldn't wait for the bathing rituals to be over. She'd talk to Pylia too and tell her to look – maybe Pylia had already noticed. To her disappointment they returned to the sleeping chambers and got ready for bed.

She looked across at Pylia who was lying in

bed across from her, munching figs. "We don't go to the shrine tonight?" She tried to hide the disappointment in her voice.

Pylia looked surprised. "No...we go only at the time of the waxing moon."

The word was unfamiliar. "The...what?"

It gave Pylia another chance to demonstrate her acting ability. She puffed out her cheeks already full of figs and pointed to her face, then she made a huge circle with her arms as if pregnant and said, "the *full* moon!"

Penny laughed in spite of herself. She lay down on the cot. This was not good news. It meant it would be several weeks before they went again. And in less than a week she was leaving Crete. She'd forgotten exactly when but she knew the holiday was nearly over.

She lay there, her eyes shut, listening to the murmur of talk from the girls in the other part of the chamber and thinking of time. She'd tried before to analyze the way time was working. It was different now with the bull bringing her back and forth than it had been when she'd come through the courtyard at the palace or with the sand from it. Then it had seemed to be passing in some sort of ratio — ten minutes of the present equalled an hour or two in the past. Now she lost no time, it seemed. She would return to the place and time that she'd left, though if she'd been sleeping it was hard to tell. But what depressed her most was that, whatever the ratio, there was definitely not enough time for her to wait for the next full moon.

Remembering that reminded her of Pylia's demonstration and she smiled and turned to her friend. Talking to Pylia always made her feel better. But Pylia was lying on her side, curled like a kitten, fast asleep.

Looking at her friend made Penny's eyes fill with tears. What if she couldn't save her? She did not want to be in the bull court the day Pylia "met her bull" even if it meant deserting the Dolphins. She touched the bull at her throat and closed her eyes.

The next thing she knew her mother was calling her. "Oh there you are, napping again."

Penny sat up quickly. The sun was still shining. She'd pulled up a sheet when she lay down in her bikini, now she peeked underneath to see what she was wearing. She'd forgotten to change again. Somewhere back in Minos' palace there was a bikini. She'd have to make at least one trip back to get it – what would the archeologists have thought to find the remnant of some synthetic garment in amongst the ruins! It was an interesting thought. But just now she had to get rid of Mum so she could change again.

"I got so drowsy sunbathing," she yawned, "but I didn't want to fall asleep and get a burn, so I came back up to lie down." She remembered her mother's reluctance to leave that morning and the realization that she was envious of Penny's leisurely day. "Say!" she said, glancing at the clock, "why don't you slip into your suit and meet me by the pool?"

Her mother's grateful, happy look made her feel a bit guilty – I've done it again, she thought – the right thing for the wrong reason! But she was relieved to be alone so quickly. Of course she wouldn't be tanning in the bikini now. Her swimsuit would have to do, but she'd do a lap or two to justify the suit and then too she could use the tan lines excuse if Mum asked any questions.

Mum was there waiting in a lounge chair when Penny arrived. "Put some lotion on my back, will you dear?" she said, holding out the bottle.

Penny obliged. Then lay back in her own chair. The sun was hot but there seemed always to be a breeze. "Mmmm, this is nice."

"Wonderful," her mother mumbled back. "I hate the thought that we have only three more days before we have to leave."

Penny sat bolt upright. "Three? Did you say we have only *three* more days?" She was horrified.

Her mother raised her head and smiled at her. "'Fraid so," she said laughing, "I take it from your reaction that you don't want to leave!"

Penny didn't answer. She lay back holding her eyes shut so her mother wouldn't see the tears. It wasn't a case of "don't want to leave" – she *couldn't* leave – yet. Now she was too depressed to even try to think of a plan. It was too late.

There was no getting out of Dad's next expedition later that afternoon either. Penny even considered pleading sick. They were off, he announced, to take the boat trip from the seaside town of Elounda to the island of Spinalonga.

Penny sat miserably in the back of the car. The hills with the snow-capped Dikti Mountains in the background were vivid with wildflowers, masses of red poppies and the yellow shrubs that had burst into bloom since their last drive this way, but she didn't care. She noticed again how few dwellings there were. Had there been even fewer in Minoan times? Lots of places to hide. *If* anyone could escape.

Even the incredible vista looking out towards the island didn't cheer her up. She followed silently as they boarded the boat. This wasn't a guided tour but Dad made up for it as he read bits from his constant companion guidebook telling them about the old Venetian fortress built in 1579 partly to protect the bay from the raids of the pirate Barbarossa, how after the country had fallen to the Turks in 1715 it became a Turkish town and the fortifications were still used until the Turks left in 1898.

"Then, until only thirty years ago, it was a leper colony!" he finished with a dramatic flourish as the boat docked.

The ancient Venetian gun turret towered above them, topped by a small Turkish building. Here too there were masses of wildflowers, the whites and yellows broken everywhere by brilliant red poppies just like the ones Penny knew at home from Remembrance Day. Appropriate, she thought. So many have died here.

"Please be back at the boat in two hours," said their captain. And pointed, "To your left is Dante's gate."

They climbed a little ways and there was the old Venetian arched entryway, its barred gateway opening into darkness beyond. It was gloomy and a little frightening in the tunnel.

"Dante's Gate?" murmured her mother, her voice echoing eerily. "Oh, of course: 'Abandon Hope All Ye Who Enter Here'"

Perhaps, Penny thought, that would have been a good sign for the bull dancers quarters at Knossos: "Abandon Hope." But she thought of Rhion standing bravely in front of the team facing the bull. And the pep talk he'd given them. She thought of Melanthro pulling her from the back of the bull and the others coming in one by one to vault the bull and distract it. They hadn't abandoned hope. And if people ever seemed to be in a hopeless situation, they were. If they'd really abandoned hope they would all have met their bull by now. Every one of them would be dead.

In the late afternoon sunshine the island

seemed to glow, the warm stones of the old
Venetian houses, later the refuge of the lepers who
had even used the giant old stone water tanks to
collect rainwater just as the Venetians had, since
there were no springs on the island.

They wandered around the island passing the
other turrets where cannons had faced out into
the bay, passing the unmarked graves of the ceme-
tery and back down to where the boat waited.
Everywhere there were flowers and birdsong.
Penny looked up as she left. There, clinging to the
side of the gun tower, a bird had built its nest. She
could see it sitting. Soon eggs would hatch, she
thought.

"Where there's life there's hope," she'd heard.
It hadn't really meant much until now, but why
else was Rhion so determined to keep the team
alive – giving them life and, somehow, hope. She
settled into the back seat as they left the lights of
Agios Nicolaos behind. If the team hadn't abandoned hope, neither would she. She couldn't wait
to get back to the hotel and hold her bull.

CHAPTER TWENTY

She wakened to find herself in the cot across from Pylia. She had no idea what time it was, but the lamps still burned as they had when she left. She could hear the girls in the outer chamber murmuring and giggling as if they had not yet fallen asleep. Her cot seemed to shake and she turned, expecting to find Pylia getting ready to bounce her, but Pylia lay sleeping, in the same kitten position. Had it been hours or minutes?

There was a surprised murmuring amongst the girls when Medusa told them to get dressed and come with her. What was it? But no one knew and the priestess merely stood by the door impatiently waiting. Were they going to the shrine? But it wasn't time. Penny wanted to ask Pylia but she was groggily getting dressed and seemed to be as puzzled as everyone else.

Once again Penny walked beside Pylia along

the corridors. It seemed they were going to the shrine of Mother Dia. And whether it was only the confusion they all felt or something else tonight, it seemed there was a closeness, a heaviness in the air that made her glad when they made their way out of the passageway beneath the palace and came at last into the open again. The palace stood across from them, torchlight soft through the open windows. But tonight they did not go to the cave with the snakes.

Tonight Medusa led them past the cave, down a path sometimes inside the rocky hillside and sometimes skirting the edge like a goat track.

"Where are we going?" Penny whispered, pretending to stumble closer to Pylia's ear.

"It looks as if they're letting us join in the dancing...to the goddess." Pylia leaned toward her. "Bull girls are usually not allowed out, except to the shrine." They looked at each other. They were out. Now there really was hope.

They followed a rocky path until they came at last to a meadow filled with women dancing and chanting in the strange guttural tongue the old priestess used. Somewhere in the centre there was a fire, but more than that Penny could not see for the bodies bobbing and weaving in the dance around it. Was this some solstice celebration to the goddess? Ahead of her the other girls began to follow the women's lead and dance too, circling around the others in the glow of the flames.

Penny looked around, trying to see where they were, whether there was any way of breaking away from the group. The path had led them away from the hillside, though she could still see it looming darkly. She could not spot the palace, although a glow she saw may have come from its lights. The trampled grasses were wet beneath her feet. They always went barefoot before the goddess.

Pylia took her hand so that she would not be left standing alone and they began to move with the dancers, swaying in rhythm to a drum someone was beating somewhere closer to the fire. Penny held onto Pylia now, afraid to be lost in the crowd of women. There must be dozens here, a hundred, even hundreds. She could smell the heavy musky perfume they oiled their bodies with and again she felt suffocated, the air closing in on her as it had in the passage.

Then it happened. First only a hint, trembling in the damp earth beneath their feet. Then a rumbling like thunder – not sky but earthborne. She broke away from the dance, grateful they were in the outer circle still, and tried to pull Pylia away from the crush of women who swayed and fell and screamed in a dance choreographed by some nightmare they all shared.

She tried to run, but it was like trying to run in molasses on the deck of a bouncing ship, and she made no headway. As soon as they were clear of the others, they fell to the ground, clinging to it as if trying to hold on. On the hillside they had just come from, rocks danced too and fell crashing down. Then there was too much dust to see anymore, and they lay side by side, afraid to move even if they could have. She lay face down in the damp earth, her arms shielding her head as the pebbles rained down.

How long the earth shook Penny could not tell. And after it was still they lay listening to the screaming, their nostrils filled with the awful smell of burnt flesh. They stood at last and looked around.

It was sheer luck that they had danced their way to the side of the meadow opposite the rocky hillside, for the rocks had tumbled in to cover over half the area – bowling the dancers over, crushing them beneath. Like a piece of the Frank slide, Penny thought. A river of rock covered the path they had walked up from the cave.

Near the fire, the women had fared even worse. Burning logs had joined the dance, flying into them, killing the lucky ones. Everywhere women beat at the flounced skirts they wore trying to put out the flames. Some ran screaming like living torches into the night.

The bull girls of their team had been luckiest. Last to the dance, they had been on the outside away from the fire and furthest from the falling stones. They gathered, frightened and weeping.

Only Charis had been hurt. Knocked down by one of the flaming women, she was bruised and slightly burned, her robe still smouldering. Penny seized handfuls of damp earth and clapped them together on the embers being careful to catch the fabric between her hands and not rub them against Charis' body and burn her again.

Like the team they were, the girls left and picked their way through the sacred grove to where they had a clear view of the palace. We're free, Penny thought. This is what I was hoping for. But as one they headed toward Knossos, where the dim glow they had seen before was brighter now. Fire! There are always fires after an earthquake. Tumbling beams would have knocked over braziers. She remembered there were places the tour guide had pointed out ancient scorch marks. She'd heard too that there were sometimes tidal waves, but she couldn't see the harbour from here.

As Penny came in sight of the palace she was surprised that there had been so little damage. Some pillars had fallen and of course there was the light of fires burning here and there, but she had expected to find the crumbled ruins that she'd seen when she visited. Worse maybe – none of Evans's reconstruction. There were areas that were crumbled and she could see from here that the stands of the bull court had fallen and the area nearby that had housed their changing rooms seemed to have caved in.

"Rhion," Penny breathed.

The girls began to run. They were athletes and showed it now – leaping fallen trees and anything in their way. They swept on towards the palace. Charis was in the lead, her mud-spattered tunic flapping about her.

They found some of the bull boys helping to fight the fire or lift pieces of pillar to look for people trapped beneath.

"Where is...where are...the others?" Penny gasped.

The others, they said, had fled. They might never have another opportunity. Even with the freedom the boys had to go about the palace, they had never been allowed outside, and so never had a chance to escape.

"They are Cretans and they are returning to their homes," Pylia explained. She looked quickly about her. "I should go too, while I can."

Penny looked startled. "You came from here?...from Crete?"

Pylia nodded. "A little farm in the Eastern hills. One of the nobles saw me doing somersaults and offered to buy me for the dance. It was an honour, though my mother wept. Now I am growing and soon I will be too tall for the dance and the bull will catch me at last."

"The bulls are gone too," Melanthro said.

Penny had not noticed him until now. He straightened from moving rubble, the muscles of his shoulders red with dust in the flickering light.

"Gone? How? What happened?" Pylia turned in disbelief. "How can the sacred bulls be gone? They are kept safe in the pasture of Poseidon." She turned and pointed to the dark hillside beyond the palace walls.

"The stone walls broke, the bulls bellowed and ran. It will be a while before they can be returned...more likely new bulls must be found. That will take time." Melanthro wiped his forehead leaving streaks of red dust like blood in the sweat.

"Then the bull dancers are free to go..." Pylia's voice was soft and she looked away eastward as if she had already left them.

"Only if they go quickly before new bulls are dedicated and the dance begins again."

Penny could bear it no longer. She could see Charis running here and there questioning people.

"Melanthro," Penny cried, "Where is Rhion? Did Rhion go too? Surely, he would not have left Charis behind!"

"No," said Pylia, "He would not have left his sister."

"Sister?" Penny breathed the word.

Pylia turned to her. "They were one birth you know."

Penny stood stunned. Twins! They were twins! No wonder they were so close. It explained why they fought with and cared for each other so much. One birth. And she'd been so jealous. "Where is he?" she screamed.

Melanthro shook his head and pointed back toward the crumbled area beside the court.

And then Penny heard Charis screaming and screaming and they were all running again.

CHAPTER TWENTY-ONE

Rhion lay where Charis had found him, his arm beneath one of the heavy wooden pillars that had fallen. Charis was pulling stones away from around his head. He was unconscious, his head was bleeding, but it looked to Penny as if he was still alive.

Melanthro and Lukos and some of the others were trying to lift the column but it was heavy, too heavy for them. Penny tore off her tunic and ripped it into strips. One of the terra cotta pipes that brought fresh water to the palace was broken. Miraculously some water still trickled through and disappeared amongst the broken paving stones. She wet the cloth and started to bathe Rhion's forehead. He was moaning now. Charis was holding his hand and all Penny could do was bend over him.

She wanted to say, "wake up," she wanted him

to stir and speak, and most of all she wanted to apologize to him for being angry that he was flirting with her when she'd thought Charis was his girlfriend. But she held back. Waking him might not be the kindest thing. He would be in pain and might struggle and make things worse.

She looked impatiently at the boys still struggling with the pillar. Melanthro had gone and was returning with Pylia. Pylia hadn't left! Penny wanted to bless her for staying a little longer. She was helping Melanthro carry a pole. Good! They would use it as a wedge beneath the pillar, with stones for a fulcrum. Penny remembered some science lesson, and her brain registered surprise at the usefulness of something she'd only memorized for a test once in another world, another time.

She watched the boys putting their weight on the pole now, held her breath as it bent and prayed that it would not break. It didn't. Little by little they lifted the pillar and held it. Not high enough. Penny moved quickly, grabbing stones to shove underneath so that the pillar would not fall back. Still there seemed to be no space between it and Rhion's arm, although it must have eased the weight on it a little.

Pylia took over from her and she left to rinse the cloth again in the cool water. This time when she placed the cloth on his forehead Rhion opened his eyes and looked at her. And smiled.

"Penelope," he said and closed his eyes again.

Penny decided that it was the most beautiful name she'd ever heard – if he said it. She'd been trying to smile back, but realized that she was crying. Not out loud but she was aware of tears dripping from her chin.

She looked over at Charis who was smiling through tears too. They would get him out. The pillar had lifted a bit more, Pylia's pile of stones underneath it was growing. The pressure on his arm must be almost gone. She hoped that they could move the pillar away somehow so that they wouldn't have to drag him out from under. His arm must be broken.

It was worse than that. She could see it, now that they had him clear. Crushed, flattened flesh with fragments of bone protruding. She wondered if even modern doctors could save it. Here it could not be saved. Rhion was one of those who would never take the bull by the horns again.

They cleaned it as best they could. She and Charis, working together. Now and then Rhion would open his eyes and smile, though the pain must have been terrible. With Melanthro's help they carried him away from the palace to the hillside – in case, just in case, someone noticed that they were bull dancers who should be locked away again.

At dawn, Charis found a village woman who bound Rhion's arm in cloth with strong smelling oil that Pylia said had come from healing herbs.

Penny hoped they would keep away infection and let the arm heal, but she saw the woman shake her head when she spoke to Charis. Penny didn't like to think of how an amputation would have to be performed here.

"I must find some way of getting him home." Charis said. She didn't ask if Penny would stay. She knew.

Pylia and Melanthro stayed too, though the other bull dancers were gone – heading homeward by any way they could find, or hiding until they could go. They learned from these people what had become of the bulls. They were told the bulls ran down to the sea and were caught in huge waves that swept the boats ashore and flooded the harbour. The villagers believed the bulls went back to Poseidon, the god who owned them.

The village women had given Pylia a bowl of broth and they fed some to Rhion, who slept fitfully. Penny remembered from somewhere in a First Aid course that people with concussions should be wakened often and so she talked to him as she continued to bathe his forehead. He would open his eyes, see her, and smile, though she knew waking brought an awareness of the pain. Sometimes he would just say her name, other times they would talk a little. He asked first how the rest of the team had fared and she told him they were all alive and going home now.

As the morning passed, Penny tried not to

think of her parents. She hoped somehow it was still night and they had not missed her.

The village woman returned, still mumbling ominously and shaking her head as she wrapped Rhion's arm again. Penny did not understand her. This must be the real Minoan language, she thought – at the palace they spoke some form of Greek. Pylia would understand what the woman had said but she looked at Pylia's worried face and did not want a translation. She clung to the knowledge that so far Rhion was not feverish so there was no infection – yet.

It was late afternoon before Charis returned. She was tired and dirty but she smiled at them. "Help me to get him to the shore. I have found a fisherman who will take us home."

Penny's relief was tinged with sorrow. It was good that Rhion would be going back to where he would be safe with people to care for him, but she knew she could not go. She had to go home too. Quickly, she tore up the last of her tunic to make a sling the way she'd learned in Girl Guides. The result wouldn't have given her a First Aid badge but it took some of the pressure off Rhion's arm. With Melanthro supporting him, Penny took the other side and Charis led the way. Pylia followed, carrying the blanket the village woman had given them in exchange for Rhion's ring.

The fishing boat was bigger than Penny expected. There were several men to row and, now that the quake was over, the sea was fairly calm. She wondered how Charis had managed to hire so many men and then saw that the jewel she'd won that first day in the bull court was gone. Charis's only badge now was her scarred shoulder.

They settled Rhion as comfortably as they could, with the blanket, on top of a pile of nets. Comfortable, Penny thought, but smelly.

He smiled at her and whispered, "Thank you, Penelope." And closed his eyes.

Penny could hardly see for tears as she and Charis hugged. "Come with us?" Charis whispered.

Penny already knew how she would handle this part. She shook her head. Then she looked towards shore. Melanthro and Pylia were walking quickly back up the hill. Penny couldn't speak so she just pointed as if she was going with them and Charis understood. "I'll say goodbye for you to Rhion," she said softly.

Then Penny left to run after Melanthro and Pylia. They were already well into an olive grove and she was breathless when she caught up to them.

"You left without saying goodbye," she accused Pylia.

Then neither of them could speak as they hugged. Penny spoke first. "You'll be all right, you can find your way home?"

"Melanthro," Pylia said, laughing, "is going to

protect me from brigands!" She looked back toward the shore. "But you'd better hurry...you're going with Rhion and Charis to their island?"

Penny turned and started to run as if she was returning to the shore. "Yes!" she called. "Going to Dia island." She pointed to the long, low-lying island she recognized from her visits to Heraklion harbour.

She could hear Pylia's laughing response. "Not Dia silly...they are from Thera!"

Penny ran until she was out of sight of them. It was only when she stood panting at the edge of the hill, watching the boat already moving strongly away from shore, that Pylia's words registered. Thera? Wasn't that Santorini's old name? Santorini – the volcanic island? How many years would it be until it was destroyed, destroying Knossos, too, for the final time? She was glad for once she didn't have her father's famous guide-book. She didn't want to know.

So they were all free. To go home. Sadly, Penny touched her bull.

CHAPTER TWENTY-TWO

Penny stood waiting for her mother in the little shop at the Heraklion Airport. As usual Dad had got them there far too early for their flight to Athens, the first lap of their journey home. She'd browsed too for awhile – picking up and putting down the varying-sized statues, "Snake Goddess, copy from the Museum." "Priestess," Penny corrected to herself every time she saw the words. Did she want a copy as a souvenir? Not really. The memory of Medusa was quite enough.

She fingered the little golden bull at her throat. She'd been rubbing it steadily ever since she returned. Nothing happened. And she knew nothing would. The bulls and their dancers were gone. Gone as far as Penny was concerned. More might come but the Dolphins were gone.

She wondered about Pylia and Melanthro. Had

they stayed together? She liked to think that they had — had farmed, had olive groves like the ones she'd seen when they drove in the hills above Mohos, high above the ancient ruins of Mallia. Loving, laughing Pylia and strong, noble Melanthro, like fairy-tale characters. She hoped they had lived happily ever after. She liked happy endings.

Thinking of them made her feel unbearably sad. Rhion was gone. How could she explain it to anyone? Here she was mourning the loss of a young man who'd probably died over three thousand, maybe four thousand years ago.

She tried to let the puzzle of time distract her. When had the earthquake happened? It was not the final one that had destroyed Knossos. There'd been a lot of damage but it could be repaired. She picked up a book, one of the tourist guidebooks on Knossos, and leafed through it. There it was: "After two partial destructions, one in 1600 and one in 1500 BC, the palaces were totally destroyed in 1450 and never rebuilt." So, Penny thought, if her earthquake was the 1500 BC one — that was three thousand five hundred years ago, give or take a few years. A long time for Rhion to be gone. A long time to mourn. He and Charis would have had fifty years before the final destruction of their island.

"How much is this book?" she asked the store owner in Greek. She fumbled in her pocket — might as well get rid of the last few drachmas.

"Hey! You speak Greek! But you read English? Good, I need a translator."

The voice was male, nearby. She'd been aware of a young man looking at the postcards but had been busy with her own thoughts. Besides she didn't want to talk to anybody just now, although his accent was familiar. She busied herself with handing over several thousand drachmas and waiting for her change. Maybe if she ignored him.

"No really. I've been here with my grand-mother visiting relatives and I don't speak any Greek...and she speaks mostly Greek especially when we're here...and..." he hesitated, aware of Penny's aloofness. "...Please?"

She raised her eyes still not looking at him. There was a Canadian flag on his backpack. Oh well, might as well show a little patriotic friendli-ness.

"Well then, what can I do...for a fellow coun-tryman...?" Penny began, and then looked in his eyes.

Soft deep brown – Rhion's eyes. She stopped and stared. His hair was dark and curly, not long like Rhion's but sort of framing his face, the way Rhion's had when it slipped out of the twisted ponytail after a handstand in the ring. She couldn't help herself, she stood rudely, staring open-mouthed.

"You're from Canada too? Cretan family background, I'll bet. And you're flying home now too? Maybe we can sit together...on the plane to Athens anyway." He stuck out his hand. "By the way, my name is Raymond, but you can call me Ray."

Wordlessly Penny took his hand and shook it.

"And you are?" he asked laughing, and then as if sharing a confidence, "You know it's customary when people are introducing themselves to give your name too!"

Penny's mouth had gone very dry and she wasn't sure if she could speak but finally managed to say very softly, "My name is Penelope." Then she realized she was still holding his hand and dropped it, feeling terribly embarrassed.

But he was turning to a grey-haired lady who'd just arrived saying delightedly, "Yia-yia, this is Penelope...from Canada!"

And then there was a blur of introductions because Mum had come over dragging Dad along and it turned out that Ray's grandmother knew Penny's great-uncle in Toronto, and there was a flurry of names and "do you knows?" and "how is's?"as the Greek connections were made. Through it all Penny stood numbly and Raymond talked of all the places they'd visited in Crete and had she liked Rethymnon?...that was where his grandmother's family had come from.

Now and then she managed to nod and acknowledge what he'd said. But mostly she just stared at him. The way he pushed his hair back from his forehead when he talked just as Rhion did. She listened without protest as he asked his grandmother to change seats with Penny on the plane.

She could hear her parents now talking with Ray's grandmother about her in that horrible embarrassing way parents have of talking about you with another older person as if you were invisible or deaf – or incredibly stupid.

But Ray just laughed. "Case history time," he said, smiling conspiratorially at her. "In a minute you'll be hearing all about me!"

She smiled at him. He had a way of making things easier. "We can handle this," his manner said. "No matter what they say about us – we're in it together. Equal time. Equal embarrassment."

He was right. The painful explanation of Penny's "illness" and trip to get her away from her "eating problems" and "brother problems" was over. And now it was Ray's grandmother's turn. Penny had made up her mind not to listen but then the words cut through and sent a chill through her.

"...terrible car accident nearly two years ago..." she heard without wanting to. Then there were more details she managed to ignore and then, "...but he's adjusted amazingly well to the artificial arm..."

Penny's face registered her shock in spite of herself. And then she felt even worse for having shown Ray her feelings. He might think it was disgust at a handicap he couldn't help. Her eyes filled with tears. But he didn't take it as disgust, maybe because of the tears.

"Hey, it's okay! I'm doing fine!" He put his arm round her and gave her shoulder a quick, familiar squeeze. Then he waved the other in front of her, moving his hand, "course I'm not doing gymnastics anymore!"

He was smiling, as if to say, "share the joke," but she couldn't. It was his left arm, she realized. It had been Rhion's left arm too.

"Listen Penelope," his voice again full of concern, "one thing all this has taught me. When something bad happens..."

It was Rhion's voice, that patient explaining voice, she was hearing again.

"When something really bad happens and you can't run away so you just have to face it...deal with it..." He paused, touched her cheek gently and smiled. "...You have to take the bull by the horns, it's the only way!"

She knew it was true. She could do it. Brothers or coaches. She'd faced worse. She suddenly felt better than she had in ages. She smiled at them all. "Do you think we have time to grab something to eat?"

BIBLIOGRAPHY FOR
THE DEADLY DANCE

Ayrton, Michael. *The Maze Maker,* Holt, Rinehart & Winston, New York, 1967.

Cottrell, Leonard. *The Bull of Minos,* Efstathiadis Group, Athens, 1994.

Cottrell, Leonard. *Digs and Diggers,* Pan Books, London, 1966.

Davaras, Costis. *Knossos and the Herakleion Museum,* Hannibal Publishing House, Athens.

Ellingham, Dubin, Jansz and Fisher. *Greece,* The Rough Guide, 1992.

Evans, Sir Arthur. *The Palace of Minos,* MacMillan, London, 1935.

Evans, Sir Arthur. *Knossos Frescos Atlas,* Gregg Press, 1967.

Graf, Fritz. *Greek Mythology,* Johns Hopkins University Press, Baltimore and London, 1996

Hall, Rosemary. *Greece,* Lonely Planet Publications, 1994.

Harrington, Spencer P. M. "Saving Knossos" *Archaeology,* January/February, 1999.

Michailidou, Anna. *Knossos, A Complete Guide to the Palace of Minos,* Ekdotike Athenon S. A., Athens, 1998.

Nelles. *Crete,* Nelles Guides, 1995.

Pendlebury, J. *The Archaeology of Crete,* Biblio & Tannen New York, 1963.

Powell, Dilys. *The Villa Ariadne,* Efstathiadis Group, Athens, 1982.

Renault, Mary. *The King Must Die,* Vintage, New York, 1988.

Renault, Mary. *The Bull from the Sea,* Penguin Books, London, 1973.

Rose, H. J. *A Handbook of Greek Mythology,* Methuen, London, 1958.

ACKNOWLEDGEMENTS:

The author gratefully acknowledges the support of The Canada Council in the writing of this book.

There are so many people to thank, all the way back to my Classics professor Robert Buck who started my fascination with ancient civilizations! Thanks to Eleni Catsoulakis, who helped me with my little bits of Greek when I was staying in Gouves, Crete. And my friends Mary and the late Michael Chryssoulakis who let me borrow their name. Thank you too to my grandchildren, Katy, Harrison and Calvin Taylor who let me play with Monty, their python, whenever I visited. I am very grateful to my wonderful editor, Geoffrey Ursell, who recognized my vision for the book and helped me so much. And to all my readers who helped with comments and advice, especially Sean Livingston, Suzanne Harris and Earl Georgas. Of course my thanks go to Earl for his love and support as I finished the book.

ABOUT THE AUTHOR

One of Canada's best-known children's authors,
Cora Taylor has published nearly a dozen juvenile
novels, including *Ghost Voyages* and *Ghost Voyages
II: The Matthew* for Coteau, *On Wings of a
Dragon, Angelique: Buffalo Hunt* and others. She
has received numerous awards and commenda-
tions for her work, and has served in writer in res-
idence positions everywhere from St. Albert,
Alberta, to Tasmania.

Cora Taylor was born in Fort Qu'Appelle,
Saskatchewan, and grew up on a farm near Fort
Carlton. After moving to Alberta, she studied
writing with the likes of W.O. Mitchell and Rudy
Wiebe. She published her first book, *Julie,* in 1985.
She continues to live and write in Edmonton.